Fifty Shades
of *Oy Vey*

A Parody

Fifty Shades of *Oy Vey*

A Parody

So erotic, you'll plotz.

E L Jamesbergstein

Alfred A Knish New York

To obtain more information about this title,
inquire about publishing rights and permissions,
or just be a noodge, contact:

eljamesbergstein@gmail.com

Alfred A. Knish
A Borscht Oy Book

ISBN: 0615864376
ISBN-13: 978-0615864372

Disclaimer: E.L. Jamesbergstein should not be confused with E.L. James, an entirely different author who spells her name with fewer letters. *Fifty Shades of Oy Vey* should not be confused with the book it parodies, *Fifty Shades of Grey.* To date, no exasperated Jewish person has ever exclaimed, "Gray!"

Printed by CreateSpace, an Amazon.com Company

CONTENTS

CHAPTER ONE

I scowl at my reflection in the window of the subway car. Damn my naturally curly dark hair. If only it would obey. I've tried so hard to whip it into shape. I've teased it and tied it up. I've used a stiff hairbrush on it. I've restrained it with bands, clips and clamps. I've slapped it with gel and smothered it with conditioner. I've even used candles, hot wax and a curling iron. Still, it's as kinky as ever. Why won't it submit to discipline?

I should be in the library, studying for final exams. Instead, I'm doing a favor for my roommate, Tiffany. She was supposed to interview a famously successful, famously secretive tycoon for the Hillel Club newsletter, but she came down with a case of acute terminal hypochondria. I have agreed to fill in. She always lets me borrow her designer clothes, so it's the least I can do.

I don't know much about Chaim Silver, founder and CEO of Silver Bagels Technology Holdings Dot Com Limited Inc., except that he's a big deal. Also, I have zero experience as an interviewer. But I know I'm smart, and how hard can this journalism thing be? To prepare, as the subway lurches from stop to stop, I'm mentally revisiting the best episodes of *The View*. That should do it.

Silver Bagels Technology Holdings Dot Com Limited Inc. occupies a full block of factory buildings in Brooklyn. A giant, gleaming stainless steel bagel on the roof guides me from the subway exit to my destination. I am, thankfully, on time.

"Anatevka Stein to see Chaim Silver," I announce to a heavy, broad-shouldered woman. Her hair is bright orange, which goes with her blouse. She beams at me with a welcoming, motherly smile.

"Chaim!" she barks, "Your 12:30 is here!"

"Thanks, Mom."

The voice that comes through the walls sounds weary. So she *is* his mother.

She turns to me and sweetly asks, "Miss Stein, can I get you something? Coffee? Tea? Some *schnecken*?"

I am lost. *Schnecken?* Is that a pastry? A dumpling? I can't remember. Damn. Journalism is harder than I thought.

"Just water," I say, playing it safe.

"One wouldn't kill you, you know," she says, sourly.

Oh no, I've offended her.

Suddenly there is activity in the hall. A bearded, scholarly-looking man is on his way out. Chaim Silver? A visitor? He looks like an elderly rabbi. He's carrying several old volumes embossed in gold with the word *Talmud*.

"Next week, we'll move on to the tractate on defilement. Keep studying!" he says, as he leaves.

"*Zey gezunt!*" says the voice from beyond the door.

"You can go in now," says Mrs. Silver.

If only I knew what to expect. Is he 30 or 60? Single or married? I guess I should have done some research instead of updating my Facebook status to "Going to meet bagel guy."

I first notice his rounded belly, extending over his belt. There's a band of baby fat around his waist, encased like a Hebrew National hot dog by a white dress shirt, buttoned up to the collar, without a necktie. There is a light dusting of dandruff on his dark suit. On his hips, *tzitzit*, the fringes worn by observant Jews, hang just so. He has a soft, gentle chin, and another soft gentle chin above that, then maybe one or two more. His hairline forms a horseshoe around a shiny bald pate, covered in part by a silver yarmulke. And between them is his pale, round, putty-colored face. Those dark black eyes.... My heart races. *Oy vey!*

I extend my hand to shake his.

"Anatevka Stein, from the Hillel newsletter," I announce. "So nice of you to see me."

"Chaim Silver," he says. "Anatevka! My favorite fictional shtetl. You intrigue me, Miss Stein."

We shake hands and my whole body tingles. He really is quite… wow.

His office is large, appointed in dark, worn furniture, with shelves containing books, a ram's horn, and commemorative plaques. Dying plants sit atop gray file cabinets. On the wall is a faded poster of the Chagall windows at The Metropolitan Opera House.

"I love Chagall," I announce.

"So you recognize his work," he says, sounding impressed. "You are most discerning, Miss Stein."

"It says, 'Chagall at The Metropolitan Opera House' on the poster," I point out.

"Yes, so it does," he agrees. "You astonish me, Miss Stein."

I am having trouble breathing. What is happening? His age and his waist size are both roughly 40. He has a pale, sickly Yeshiva boy glow. Yet I am drawn to him. Powerfully drawn to him.

"Who was that man who just left?" I ask.

"My Talmud instructor," he says. "A great man. Knows everything. This week, we did forbidden relations. Next week, defilement. Madonna uses him too."

"Shall we, um, shall we begin the interview?" I stammer.

He takes a seat behind his desk.

"What's your favorite color?"

He looks perplexed. Damn. I should have slowly worked up to that question. What would Joy Behar have asked?

I try again.

"You've had a great deal of success in business. To what do you attribute it?"

"An excellent question, Miss Stein. Some people say that business is about people. I say it's about bagels. How a bagel should taste, how dense a bagel should be, how big to make the hole in the middle of the bagel. Bottom line, it comes down to bagels. Bagels, bagels, bagels. And I know bagels."

He speaks in a singsong, nasal tone. His arrogance is off-putting, yet intoxicating.

"Humble, aren't we?"

"I was the first to see the potential of the custom online bagel," he says. "Why should you have to have an 'everything' bagel if you only wanted some things? Say you want salt and onion but no garlic—is that such a crime? I didn't start with much, just some water, yeast and flour. Of course there was some seed capital too—poppy, sesame, caraway, a little sunflower. Now we're the dominant player in bagels. Soon we'll be dominant in bialys, challahs, pumpernickel, and sponge cake."

"Being dominant is important to you?"

"Yes, Miss Stein," he says solemnly, "*Oy*, you have no idea."

So. A control freak! And yet, for some reason, I am totally turned on.

"Do you think that you are heartless?"

This is what Barbara Walters would ask. I'm sure of it.

"Have you been talking to my Mother? Every five minutes, more complaints, more *kibitzing*. I can never do enough."

"But you are a very tough businessman."

"No, I just have high standards. If we sell a hard, tasteless bagel, a lot of breakfasts will be ruined. People will suffer. I couldn't live with that."

So he has a compassionate side after all. Chaim Silver cares.

"Why bagels?" I ask.

"Why not bagels?" he replies.

"Touché, Mr. Silver." So he's witty too!

"Are you gay, Mr. Silver?" I ask.

"Me, a *feygele*?" I have wounded him. "You really have been talking to my mother. Just because I'm not married at 40! I happen to be very busy with my work and, um, private activities."

I apologize for asking, but I'm glad I did. Single and straight. Yay! But what are these private activities?

"You're notoriously private, you've refused to grant interviews to *Time* magazine, *The New York Times*, *The Wall Street Journal*. Why would you talk to a young, inexperienced, female reporter who's still in college?"

He looks into my eyes. Actually, he seems to be looking a little lower than my eyes.

"I like to help young people, Miss Stein. Tell me, you have plans after graduation? Have we got a great internship program here at Silver Bagels! We'd work closely, you and I, one-on one. You'd start at the bottom, but you get a chance to experience what it's like at the top. It's an opportunity to try out many different positions."

He is grinning. What a generous offer. How cool that he wants to boost my career. But have to disappoint him.

"No, thanks, I have plans after college."

"How about Saturday night?"

"Studying for exams."

"You are most beguiling, Miss Stein," he says, transfixing me with his small dark eyes.

"Chaim, your one o'clock is here. And you haven't had lunch!" barks a voice through the walls.

"I'm busy here, Mom," he yells back, exasperated.

"I'm sorry," he says, turning to me. "We need to wrap this up."

I thank him for his valuable time.

"Oh yes, we'll need a photo."

"Of course, he says. My mother will give you one. She always has a few handy. Also, here, please take my card. It has all my information. Call anytime."

I feel his clammy, pudgy palm as we shake hands goodbye. It's electrifying, like the time I touched a jellyfish and had to apply ointment for a week. I really must leave, but his black eyes hold me spellbound. Try to resist, I tell myself. Can I?

"*Zey gezunt*, Miss Stein," he says.

"Goodbye, Mr. Silver."

CHAPTER TWO

"How did it go?" Tiffany asks.

She is sipping chicken soup from Zabar's, sent by her doting Dad, a prominent Park Avenue dentist/gynecologist.

"He is very… well, he was so… you know."

I am blushing.

"I see," she says with a sly smile. "Sounds like it went well!"

Tiffany can be so annoying!

"Did you remember to get a photo? I'd like to see what he looks like."

I hand her the photo.

"What is this? A bar mitzvah photo?"

"His mother gave it to me," I answer. "She said he was a beautiful child."

"Chaim gave me his card," I mention. "We could call him and ask for a different photo."

She looks at the card.

"This has all of his numbers. He must like you."

I dismiss her with a shake of my head.

"Men have given me their numbers before."

"He included his American Express Card account number."

That does seem odd.

"But what could he possibly see in me? I'm just a young, inexperienced, yet sexually curious college senior."

She is staring at me.

"I know, I'm naturally thin without diet or exercise, my complexion is effortlessly flawless, and my firm yet supple breasts have been likened to the Michelin Man. But why would any of that matter?"

"We should talk," she says.

"I can't," I tell her. "I have to work."

CHAPTER THREE

Three afternoons a week, I work at a Kleinman's Hardware & Supplies, a store catering to Jewish do-it-yourselfers. Our motto: "We're not sure what we sold you. You're not sure how to use it."

I'm at the front counter, but business is slow. I look up and find myself gazing into the small black eyes of... Chaim Silver. What is he doing here? I am *so* not prepared.

He looks relaxed in his rumpled dark suit, his white shirt buttoned all the way up to the collar. He has that light dusting of dandruff on his shoulders, and his *tzitzit* hang from his hips just so. *Oy vey!*

"Miss Stein! Who knew?"

He is staring at my boobs. My nipples are tingling. Through my taut bra, they are staring back.

"Mr. Silver," I gasp. "What a surprise!"

"I needed a few things and happened to be nearby. And you—here. Go know! A *mechaya*, let me tell you."

He speaks with a rising and falling, singsong inflection, high-pitched yet not too squeaky. I can barely swallow.

Taking a deep breath, I ask him how I can help him.

"Some rope, you have, maybe?" he asks, not taking his gaze off me.

"That would be Aisle 8, Chain & Rope."

"You have chains too?" he says. "Great! Those I need also. And duct tape."

"Duct tape is in Aisle 10, Heating, Venting & Cooling. Is there anything else I can help you with?" I ask him.

"Yes. You have vibrating dildos in a range of sizes?"

"Aisle 15, Screws and Plugs."

"And maple syrup?"

"Same aisle, next to the edible panties."

I watch him make his selections.

"I didn't realize you were such a do-it-yourselfer!" I exclaim.

He can probably tell I'm nervous. Damn. I can't help it. He is just so… Ashkenazic.

"I didn't realize you were such a hardware expert," he counters.

His rapier wit unnerves me. Advantage Silver.

"I'm not," I tell him. "I'm much more of a book person. British novels, mostly. Women writers. The classics."

"Jane Austen? The Brontes?" he asks. "*Oy*, could those lady writers write!"

"No, not those. The modern classics. You know, *Confessions of a Shopaholic*, *Bridget Jones's Diary*. I'm writing my senior thesis on dieting and binge drinking as a metaphor for dieting and binge drinking."

"You are a marvel, Miss Stein."

"Incidentally," I ask, "do you have another photo we could use for the Hillel newsletter? Something more recent than from your bar mitzvah? If you don't, we have a photographer who could take one."

"A new photo, free? If you're offering, I'm accepting."

"How about this weekend?"

"Nothing would give me greater pleasure," he says, gazing deeply into my eyes.

"Great! Sunday afternoon at Mt. Carmel Zion Sinai Kosher Catering? Our photographer will be there. He'll be ready right after the Cohen wedding."

"I'm invited to that wedding! What *mazel*. I will see you there, Miss Stein."

CHAPTER FOUR

I sleep poorly that night, dreaming of small black eyes, potbellies, fringes hanging off the hips, and dark, moist, pumpernickel. I wake twice, gasping and perspiring. *Oy vey.* If I don't get some sleep, tomorrow's photo shoot is going to be a disaster.

And yet, it goes better than expected. Mt. Carmel Zion Sinai Kosher Catering is on a mostly residential street in Brooklyn. Chaim has already arrived. Everyone knows him. In the world of Jewish bagelry, he is a celebrity.

"This is fantastic," says the wedding photographer when I find him.

In the high-ceilinged banquet hall, guests have formed a circle and are clapping and stomping rhythmically as a band plays a spirited tune. At the center, beaming a broad smile, arms folded, knees bent and legs kicking, is Chaim.

"The kazatsky," says the photographer. "A traditional Russian dance."

For a rotund businessman of 40, he's light on his feet. When the music finally dies out, Chaim straightens up to his full height of 5'6" and walks toward us. Holy Moses! He's wearing his trademark white shirt, buttoned all the way up with no necktie, a dark flannel suit, and he's sweating. His shirt is moist and sticking to his belly. My mouth goes dry. He is so freaking Semitic.

"Miss Stein, we meet again." Silver extends a soft, sweaty hand, and I shake it, blinking rapidly. I'm breathless!

"Thank you for taking the time to do this," I say.

"Ach, a pleasure," he answers, turning his black eyes on me. "As long as I can be with you."

What a charmer Mr. Chaim Silver is! I can't stop blushing, damn it.

At his side is a wiry, muscular young man in his thirties, with Mediterranean looks—aquiline nose, short curly hair and olive skin.

"This is my personal assistant Schneider. He's ex-Mossad. Trained in counter-terrorism, personal protection, hand-to-hand combat, and electronic surveillance. He takes care of all my dry cleaning."

"Schneider, you can go now," he says, addressing him. "I'll call you when I need my shirts picked up."

Chaim turns to me. "A little dessert perhaps you'll have? Come, join me."

Heart pounding I agree and he leads me to a dessert buffet.

"Coffee? Tea?" he asks.

"Coffee is fine, I don't really like tea."

"How fascinating! You are most mysterious, Miss Stein."

He selects several pastries for himself, which he begins eating simultaneously.

"So, *nu,* a nice Jewish girl like you, you have a boyfriend?" he asks, crumbs falling from his mouth.

The question catches me off guard.

"No," I answer honestly. "Do you have a girlfriend?" I ask.

"No, Miss Stein. Girlfriends are not for me," he says, smirking "Not my *shtick.*"

Girlfriends not his *shtick*? What does that mean? He's not gay. Is he celibate? Too attached to his mother? Crazy ideas pop into my head. What if he's into all sorts of creepy fetishes? What if he only enjoys tying women up and degrading them sexually in a secret custom-designed dungeon in his home?

Get a grip, Anatevka, I tell myself. Don't be ridiculous.

I should ask him more about this girlfriend thing. Or maybe not. Why do I care so much?

Just then, the band starts to play *"Hava Nagila."*

"Laters, *tsatskeleh*," he announces.

Chaim jumps up and, before I know it, he has joined a line of people dancing the *hora*. I watch for a bit, feeling foolish. Then I make my way home.

CHAPTER FIVE

My last final exam is over. I'm in my apartment, brushing my hair, which is as twisted and kinky as ever. Tiffany and I are about to go out and celebrate over cosmopolitans when the doorbell rings. It's FedEx, with a package for me. What could this be?

I open the parcel. Inside is a softcover book, its colorful glossy cover marred by a few abrasions and creases: *Bridget Jones's Diary.* Pretty old, in decent shape for a used paperback, and I know immediately who sent it. Written on a plain white card is:

> I will not fall for any of the following: alcoholics, workaholics, commitment phobics, people with girlfriends or wives, misogynists, megalomaniacs, chauvinists, emotional fuckwits or freeloaders, or perverts.

I recognize the passage from the novel. I've just spent hours working on my metaphor paper. I wonder why Chaim picked this particular quote. What could it possibly mean?

I inspect the book closely.

Picador 1996.

Tiffany is at my shoulder gazing at the book. She picks up the card.

"First edition," I whisper.

"No!" Tiffany's eyes are wide with disbelief. "Chaim Silver?"

I nod. His black eyes and rotund physique have haunted my dreams. And now he sends me this. I thought girlfriends weren't his shtick. Maybe he just likes giving presents?

"Has to be."

Tiffany is looking at her iPhone. "Here's one on Amazon.com for $.01. But yours is in slightly better condition. Probably cost a little more. What's the card about?" she asks.

"It's from the beginning, where she vows not to date any jerks, although she goes on to do exactly that."

"I know," says Tiffany. "I saw the movie. So what is he saying?"

"If only I knew."

Chaim is so enigmatic! I will have to ask.

I shrug and we laugh and head out for drinks. At the bar, we toast to life after college when we will move into the chic bohemian loft Tiffany's dentist/gynecologist father just bought her and spend our entire starting salaries on cosmopolitans.

I've had several too many when I look at my phone. I drunkdial Chaim.

"Hey!"

He answers testily. "Who is calling please?"

"It's me, Ana!" I yell into the phone above the bar's din.

"Ah, Miss Stein. So nice to hear from you. Where are you?"

Why does he sound so concerned?

"Thanks for the book!" I shout.

"Ana, I can barely hear you."

"Thank you for the book!" I shout again.

"Ana… are you *farschnickert*?" he asks.

"Fa-what?"

"*Farschnickert*. Drunk. You sound like you're drinking."

"Don't go all Yiddish on me, *bubbeleh*," I reply. I must be *farschnickert* after all. "Why did you send me the book?" I ask.

"It's very loud where you are. Where is it exactly?"

"Who wants to know?" I ask.

21

"I do. A nice Jewish girl like you, you shouldn't be at such a place. If I were there right now, I'd take you over my knee and give you such a *zetz* your tushy would be sore for a week."

"Seriously? Well, in that case...."

I give him the address. Definitely *farschnickert*.

"I'm coming to get you," he says and hangs up.

Seconds, minutes, maybe hours pass—I'm not sure. My head is spinning uncomfortably. Why can't I toss these cosmos back like the girls on *Sex in the City*? When I look up, Chaim Silver and his identical twin have arrived at my table. I had no idea! No wait, I'm seeing double.

"Peach schnapps," he says to the waiter, "with two cherries. Dirty."

"And for you sir?" the waiter asks.

"That *is* for me," he explains.

"Shall we dance?" I say cheekily. "Just once. Pleez?"

He is glowering at me.

We step onto the dance floor. Chaim moves like a panda in his dark suit and white shirt as Kanye West blares from the speakers. He soon collides with a nearby couple.

"What are you doing?" I shout at him.

"The rhumba!" he shouts back.

"I'm nauseous!" I announce. The sensation has crept up on me and suddenly I have to get some air.

I leave the dance floor and weave through the crowded bar as quickly as possible. He follows me. Outside, on the street, I vomit spectacularly, doubled over, stomach heaving.

"Miss Stein, as ever, you surprise and beguile me," he says.

"I'm sorry," I mutter.

The last things I hear before I pass out in Chaim Silver's arms are his words:

"Oy vey."

CHAPTER SIX

It's morning. I'm in a bed, in my underwear. It's not my bed. I have no idea where I am. Some nice Jewish girl.

"Good morning, Anatevka. How are you feeling?"

Oh no. Chaim! How did this happen?

"Did you undress me?" I whisper.

"*Tstastkeleh*, you were kind of a mess. You wanted I should let you sleep that way?"

It's all coming back to me. "We didn't—?"

He shakes his head. "No, no, what do you take me for?"

He opens a brown paper bag. I can smell the fresh bagels.

"You need to eat. This is our newest product, the Hangover Bagel, with aspirin built in. It's going to be huge. Try one, you'll feel better."

He is so relaxed, so confident, the ruler of his

empire. Can I really be in the bed of this powerful, paunchy bagel god?

"Eat your bagel," he says. "I have to go put on *tefillin*."

I get out of bed just as he returns. I'm standing there, in my underwear, my legs scandalously bare.

"Your clothes were a mess, so I got some new things for you," he says, handing me a bag. "From T.J. Maxx. Hope they fit. I don't think they can be returned."

In the bathroom, I strip off my clothes and climb into the shower. Do I want Chaim Silver? Yes, my inner yenta answers. I want to feel his hands and his mouth on me, his convex hairy belly pressing against me, his pale flesh touching mine, his vast wealth and my tiny NOW account, together, intertwined in a passionate embrace.

"Why didn't you take advantage of me last night?" I ask when I'm dressed.

"Well," he says. He turns the word into three syllables with his unique, nasal whine. "There are some things we need to do first. Some paperwork."

He is smiling at me.

"What does that mean?"

"Exactly what it sounds like, my little *hamentaschen*. I need to show you, but not now. I have to go to the plant. We're getting some new bialy machines. Are you free tonight?"

"Yes, I think so."

"OK, you want I should come by you and pick you up? How about 8PM?"

"That will be fine," I say and make my way to the door.

"Schneider will get Sidney Cha-Cha fueled and ready. Laters, *tsatskeleh*!"

Sidney Cha-Cha?

CHAPTER SEVEN

I'm all nerves and anticipation, waiting for Chaim. As always, I am wearing my roommate's clothes. Tiffany doesn't mind at all, and she especially likes having them dry cleaned later.

Chaim arrives punctually. He opens the passenger door to a silver Oldsmobile Delta 98, and I clamber in.

"Come aboard," he says. "Welcome to Sidney Cha-Cha."

His car has a name!

It's huge with a silver-gray vinyl roof and interior. Holy Moses. I've seen cars like this in movies, but never thought I would ride in one. The car rocks like a boat as we pull away from the curb, then settles as we reach cruising speed.

"350 cubic inch V-8 engine Power steering and brakes, tilt wheel and cruise control, AM/FM stereo with 8-track tape deck, the whole *shmear*," Chaim informs me.

"What are we listening to?" I ask aloud.

"The Barry Sisters. '*Bei Mir Bist Du Sheyn*.' You like?"

"It's, um, very nice."

"It is, isn't it?" he grins, glancing at me. He seems happy. I sink back into the deep leather seats and listen to the sisters' voices, serenading me in Yiddish.

"What else do you listen to?"

"I got everything, from Barry Manilow to Barbra Streisand. It depends on my mood. And you?"

"Who is Barry Manilow?" I ask. I have a lot to learn about music.

He turns and gazes at me briefly before his eyes are back on the road. The massive car swerves and nearly takes out a street lamp.

I grip the door. Does this car have air bags? I don't think so.

Tires squealing, we run a red light.

Oy vey.

"Maybe you should get a helicopter," I say. "Then you wouldn't have to worry about curbs and traffic signals."

"Don't be a wisenheimer. Those things are dangerous. I don't even fly commercial. Thank *G-d* for Greyhound."

My heart is racing as we fly through the streets.

Miraculously we make it to Chaim's home off Ocean Parkway in one piece. Schneider opens the door for us. It's a two family home, Chaim explains, which he shares with his parents. Schneider lives in a spare room in the basement.

"Your Mom is downstairs? And Schneider too?" I guess I should be worried. "How convenient for you," I say.

"I'm going to have a drink. You'll join me?"

"Yes, please." I murmur. After riding in Sidney Cha Cha, I could use two.

I am standing in his living room. There is a black leather sectional sofa, a large glass coffee table covered with books about Israel, and an étagère filled with tchotchkes. The rust-colored rug has a colorful, geometric pattern.

"Peach schnapps okay with you?"

"Sounds fine."

My heart is pounding. I shouldn't have come here. This is a mistake. But my inner yenta rolls her eyes at me and tells me to grow up. She's excited.

"Here."

He hands me a small, stemmed glass of the liqueur. The schnapps is so sweet and cloying I can only sip a little.

"*L'chaim*," he says. "Can I offer you a little chopped liver?"

I shake my head.

"No, I'm not really hungry."

"So?" he says, chomping on chopped-liver and pumpernickel. "Why should that matter?"

I am hungry for something, or at least my inner yenta is. Looking around the room, I point to the accordion sitting on the table.

"Do you play?"

"Yes."

"Are you good?"

"I've played a few *simchas* in my day."

"Of course you have. Is there anything you don't do well?"

"Quite a few, *tsatskeleh*. Fly fishing, polo, transmission repair." He takes a sip of schnapps.

"Why did you give me *Bridget Jones's Diary*?" I ask.

Chaim stares at me.

"Between me and you, I enjoyed it. That part with her and the bunny costume at the party—funn-ee! What's not to like?"

He is so literary!

"Are you Daniel Cleaver or Mark Darcy?" I ask. Cleaver, the disappointing cad or Darcy, her true love. "Or maybe you're the creepy uncle, always trying to cop a feel?"

"*Oy*, I didn't know there would be a quiz. Which one davens more?"

I am bewitched by his charm. Our eyes lock. My mouth is dry.

"Are we going to make love tonight, Mr. Silver?"

Holy Moses. Did I just say that? His mouth drops open slightly, but he recovers quickly.

"*Gevalt!* No, Miss Stein, Anatevka, sweetheart. First, I don't make love. I *shtup*. I *shtup* hard.

Second, there's the paperwork. I told you. Nothing happens without the paperwork. You've heard of Levine, Levine & Levine? My attorneys. They've got to review everything.

And third, you need to visit the playroom, so you know what's what. This is not *pisha paysha*."

My inner yenta is confused. Levine, Levine & Levine. Three Jewish lawyers are involved? That sounds so... hot! I am trembling with excitement. But why must we visit a playroom? He's 40 and he doesn't have kids. And what is *pisha paysha*?

CHAPTER EIGHT

The first thing I notice about the playroom is the *mezuzah*. Then the smell: faintly acrylic, not altogether unpleasant. I see a large Chesterfield couch protected by clear plastic slipcovers. The floor is covered in lush blue wall-to-wall carpeting.

There is a gigantic wooden Star of David fastened to the wall. It's made of highly polished mahogany, and there are restraining cuffs on the points of the star. Above it, an iron grid is suspended from the ceiling, and from it hang all manner of ropes, chains and shackles. Plus a pine tree-shaped air freshener. There is an enormous bed covered in blue-tinted leather, no sheets or blankets, though there is a needlepoint pillow that says "Chaim." Following my gaze he explains, "From my mother."

On the far side of the room, the exact same thing—almost like a mirror image. There are two of everything!

"This side is for meat, that side is for dairy," he explains. "It's not always just whips and handcuffs.

Sometimes there's food involved. Whipped cream, brisket, you know. Must be kept separate."

"Brisket?"

"This is a dark path I'm leading you down, *tsatskeleh*," he says with a smirk.

"A dark blue broadloom path," I counter.

"*Oy*, Miss Stein, you are such a wisenheimer!" he counter counters.

CHAPTER NINE

"You must have questions, yes?" he says.

We are back in the living room.

"You mentioned paperwork."

"Yes."

"What paperwork?"

"Well, a contract saying what we will do, what we won't do, what the limits are. You know, like a *ketubah* but... kinky. We get it done in calligraphy by a *sofer,* and it's witnessed. There have to be two people not party to the sex who also sign."

"That sounds bizarre."

It's so strange I feel I should say something, and I do. "How did you get this way?"

"*Oy.* It started in summer camp. I'd tell you everything right now, but I need to drag this out as long as possible. This is going to be a trilogy, at least. A real *megillah.* Shouldn't we at least wait until Volume Two?"

"So meanwhile, we can't just make love like two normal people?"

"Ach, *tsatskeleh*, I just don't do plain vanilla. Not my thing."

"Can we talk about it?"

"No, my little pierogi, not yet. I told you, it's too soon. Maybe I'll dish a little in a few chapters."

"Okay, okay. So what are these rules that I have to follow?"

"I've got them written down. I'll show you, we'll talk. Are you sure you won't have some chopped liver?"

Food. How can I eat now?

"I'm really not hungry," I whisper, though I try a tiny morsel.

"So? You have to eat," he says simply. "You're a growing girl."

"I'm 21, I don't think I'm growing anymore."

"At least you're legal," he says. "Would you like another glass of schnapps?"

"No, thanks."

He pours himself one and comes to sit beside me.

"Why me?" I ask.

"Why not you?"

As always, he is too clever for me.

His expression is dark, deep, reflective.

"There's a special something about you, *tsatskeleh*. Possibly it's your tits."

He likes my tits! My inner yenta sings *"Hava Nagila."* This pudgy, lecherous millionaire wants me!

"Please, have a little chopped liver," he pleads.

"No."

"Such a waste. In that case, I'll wrap it up and you'll take it with you. You can have it tomorrow, it shouldn't be a total loss."

I roll my eyes and follow him into his study. He hands me a document.

"This is what I mean by rules. Just to give you an idea. For you, we'll come up with a special agreement you're guaranteed to love. Take a look."

RULES

1. Obedience:
The Submissive shall obey any instructions given by the Dominant without being a wisenheimer.

2. Food:
A latte and a Luna Bar are not a meal. The Submissive shall eat regularly and finish her plate. She shall eat from a prescribed list of foods including but not limited to:

Blini
Blintzes
Borscht
Cholent
Coffee rings
Falafel
Farfel
Gefilte fish
Gribbenes
Herring
Hummus
Kasha
Kichel
Knishes
Kreplach
Kugel
Pickled beets
Pickled herrings
Pickles
Smoked salmon
Smoked sable
Smoked whitefish
Stuffed cabbage
Stuffed kishkas
Stuffing

3. Clothes:

The Dominant shall provide a clothing budget for the Submissive. The budget shall be low, but submissive shall take advantage of sales and bargains and never pay retail.

4. Exercise:
The submissive shall kegel constantly.

5. Sleep:
The submissive shall go *shluffy* when she is told to so as not to ruin her complexion.

6. Personal Safety:
The Submissive shall not drink to excess, smoke, take recreational drugs, or put herself in any unnecessary danger. Unnecessary danger includes, but is not limited to: riding horses, climbing step ladders, eating sushi, or going out in the sun without sun block, an umbrella, and a pith helmet.

7. Personal Qualities:
The submissive shall be a Nice Jewish Girl.

8. Touching
The Submissive shall not touch the Dominant on his chest. The Submissive shall not find out why until the sequel.

9. Safewords
a. The Dominant and the Submissive recognize that, during role-play, the Dominant may make demands that the Submissive cannot meet. In such circumstances, the Submissive may make use of a "safeword," to be selected by the parties. In role play, "no" shall mean "yes," unless "no" has been designated as the safeword, in which it shall mean "no." "Yes" shall mean "yes," unless it has been

designated as the safeword, in which case it then means "no." If "yes" has been designated as a safeword and means "no," saying "no" shall still mean "yes," not "no," unless "yes" and "no" are both safewords. See section (b.) below.

b. When selecting a safeword, the parties shall try to avoid "yes" and "no."

10. Hard Limits
No camping. No do-it-yourself lawnmower repair. No hunting. No big dogs. No hang gliding. No holiday songs mentioning mangers. No going out in the cold with damp hair.

11. Penalties
The Submissive's violation of any of the foregoing will result in an immediate tushy spanking or more severe punishment to be determined by the Dominant.

Oy vey!

"How about you, *tsatskeleh*? Do you have any hard limits?"

"Hard limits?" I ask.

"What you won't do, what I won't do. *Fershtay?*"

"I don't like being tickled. Other than that, I don't really know."

"What do you mean you don't really know?"

I stare at my feet.

"Well… I haven't had sex before, so I'm not sure."

Chaim's eyes pop open wide, his moist pink lips quiver. Holy Moses. I hope he's not having some sort of attack.

"Never?" he asks.

I shake my head.

"You've never been *shtupped*?"

I nod, flushing again.

"No *shtupping* ever? Completely *unshtupped*? *Shtupping* is foreign to you? With respect to *shtupping*, you—"

"I'm a virgin!" I shout.

He closes his eyes.

"*Oy vey. Tsatskeleh*, why didn't you say something? This changes everything."

CHAPTER TEN

"Come," he murmurs.

"What?"

"I'm going to do you a huge favor."

"What do you mean?"

"Anatevka, I'm going to *shtup* you, now."

My inner yenta swoons.

"Even though I haven't signed anything? I thought you didn't do plain vanilla. What about Levine, Levine & Levine?"

He smiles benignly

"Just this once we'll make an exception. It's a sacrifice on my part, but I think you deserve it. Don't even thank me."

I try to speak, but I can't. Even my inner yenta is uncharacteristically quiet.

"We'll start with the basics," he says. "It's like learning to pray in Hebrew. One step at a time. *Bensching, yentzing*, it's all the same."

We are in his bedroom. He holds some clothes in his arms. "Undress and put this on," he says, handing me a coarse white linen gown. Then he leaves the room.

When he returns, he's wearing a linen bed shirt that doesn't quite cover his pale white thighs. He places a sheet over me. My inner yenta nudges me to complain.

"Hey, there's a hole in this sheet."

Chaim ignores me. He's busy squinting and mumbling something mysterious.

"Are you praying?" I ask.

"No. I'm reading the expiration date on the condom package. Looks like these are good till *Tishrei*, 5776."

"When is that?" I wonder as he tears open the package. Judaism is so mysterious.

Chaim climbs onto the bed, on top of the sheet.

"I'm going to take you now."

"Take me where?" I don't feel dressed for anything.

Deftly, he spreads my knees apart and suddenly he is on top of me and, through the hole in the sheet, inside me. *Oy vey!*

Chaim's whole body is shaking. He's breathing very hard.

"Ana!" he cries out. "Ah! *Oy! Oy oy oy!*"

"Are you okay?" I ask. This doesn't sound good.

"Chaim?"

He shouts one very loud *"Oy vey!"* and collapses on top of me. The pressure of his full weight pinning me to the bed leaves me panting for air.

For a moment, there is only the sound of breathing.

"Are we done?" I ask.

"*Oy*, you want even more?"

He's taking deep, gasping breaths. "You flabbergast me, Anatevka!" he says. "But you sound tired, my little knish. We'll take a break."

I stare at the ceiling. So I've had sex—and with Chaim Silver! Though it's not quite what I was expecting. My inner yenta is giving sex a bad review on Yelp. I lie there, in the darkness, and close my eyes.

When I awake, two hours have passed and Chaim is nowhere to be seen. I hear music—the lilting notes of a sad, sweet lament. It sounds familiar.

I wrap the sheet around me and quietly pad down the corridor to the living room. Chaim is there, in his bed shirt, playing the accordion, the sorrowful melody giving voice to his deep inner sadness.

"That's a beautiful piece, I say. What is it?"

"Hammlisch's 'The Way We Were.' Originally for Streisand but transcribed."

"Exquisite. But so very sad."

"Yes, Ana. So it is," he says. He stops playing and draws me to him. Chaim Silver. What a talented, tormented, accordion-playing genius.

We go back to bed together and I close my eyes once more. As sleep washes over me once more, the sorrowful strains of "The Way We Were" echo in my ears.

CHAPTER ELEVEN

Light fills the room. I stretch and open my eyes. It's a beautiful morning. Wow, what a view. Bare trees covering snowy white hills almost like hair. Oh wait that IS hair. Beside me, Chaim is fast asleep. I'm staring at his pale, fleshy, furry belly. *Oy vey.* So much to think about.

Slipping out of bed, I find his white shirt on the floor and put it on. It's like wearing a poncho. I walk through a door thinking that it might be the bathroom, but I'm in a large walk-in closet. Rows and rows of dark suits and white shirts, all identical. Chaim is so organized!

Holy Moses, I'm hungry.

His kosher kitchen daunts me. I will probably be struck by lighting if I take a fork from the wrong drawer. Still, I love to cook, and I'm pretty good at it, so I'm going to make something. I know... toast.

I'm grinning as I work. I came here to make love to Chaim Silver. Mission accomplished! But my inner yenta scowls at me. That was *shtupping*- not lovemaking, she insists. She has a point. I shake my head and concentrate on the task at hand.

"Good morning, *tsatskeleh*!"

I hear Chaim come in and I glance up.

"Toast?" I offer.

"There's an old Yiddish saying. A young woman needs a thick sausage and hard eggs."

"Not me. I'm not really into big breakfasts."

"Just a little nosh?" Why is he winking and smirking? Chaim is such an enigma! Then I look at his bed shirt. The front is tented like the corner of a *huppah* at a Jewish wedding.

"Oh!" I think. And then, "Ah." Sausage. Of course. And then, *"Oy vey!"*

"Come to me, my little honey cake," he says.

This is my first time on a person. In Jewish summer camp, we practiced on bananas. Thank *G-d* I had a little religious training.

I lift his shirt and take him in my mouth.

"Oy, does that feel good!" he moans.

My inner yenta is *kvelling*. I can do this!

I run my tongue around the peak of his miniature Mount Sinai. I'm learning so much about the Oral Law. I decide to see if I can fit both of his balls in my mouth at once. Yay!

I always knew I had a secret talent that would emerge one day. I was hoping for a photographic memory. Instead, it's my lack of a gag reflex. Who knew?

I pull him deep into my mouth, so deep that I can feel him at the back of my throat. But there is a noise outside the room.

"Chaim!" a voice calls sharply.

Chaim and I freeze. It's Chaim's Mom, Mrs. Silver. What is she doing here?

I hear another, softer voice. "He's still in bed."

Schneider! Thank G-d, Schneider will keep her out. If anyone can do it, he can. He was in the Israeli Army and the Mossad. Once, armed only with a falafel cart, he stopped an entire Syrian tank column.

"My Chaim? In bed at this hour? The boy must be unwell."

"I'm sorry Mrs. Silver."

"Schneider, you cannot keep a mother away from her son. Does he have a fever?"

"Mrs. Silver, he's not alone."

"He sent for someone before his own mother?" she wails.

The door bursts open.

"Ma!" Chaim shouts.

"Chaim?" she says, weakly.

Chaim says nothing.

"Mmmrmwrfg," I interject.

My inner yenta is confused. I should apologize. No, she should apologize. No, me. No, her. This is so awkward!

"Miss Stein... Chaim!"

Please don't let her have a heart attack, I think. Luckily, she just looks at me and then looks away. Some nice Jewish girl I am.

Then she takes in the whole the room with a despairing expression.

"Even when he was growing up, his room was always a mess. He never put anything away. A *shanda*. Chaim! How can you have company here?"

She turns to me.

"All these years, I thought he didn't like girls," she says. "I hired a matchmaker. Chaim made excuses. I set up dates for him with the daughters of friends. He wouldn't go."

Her voice is faltering.

"He was always by himself, first with his school projects, then his bagels. And now, finally, I find the two of you, here, like this. *Baruch hashem*!"

Weeping, she embraces me, crushing me into her fur coat.

"How can I ever thank you?" she says.

She is sobbing! Then she gets a grip on herself and whispers in my ear.

"He's not bi, is he?"

CHAPTER TWELVE

The phone rings twice and we can hear Schneider answer. He knocks on the door.

"Schneider, what is it?" Chaim snaps.

"Mr. Silver, there's an issue with the Darfur shipment."

Chaim picks up an extension and barks into it. Arrangements are made. Ultimatums are given. Curses are shouted.

"A plague on them!" I hear Chaim saying. "Forget the rugelach. Double the poppy seed. Make sure there's cream cheese. And tell those *mamsers* to use refrigerated trucks. *Fershtay?*" He hangs up.

Boy is he mad!

"A cholera to their bones!" he adds to no one in particular.

He looks at me with the dark eyes of a cold, calculating merchant of bagels. Yet there is kindness there too.

"You're quite the businessman," I tell him.

"You and I have some business too." He smirks.

I know he means the kinky *ketubah*. I promise him I will think about it.

"There's so much I don't know!" I tell him.

"Ach, you're a smart girl," he assures me. "Do some research, consider my offer, and we'll talk *tachlis*."

I leave laden with doubts, legal documents and leftover chopped liver.

Tiffany is in the living room when I get back.

"Well, how was it?" she asks

"It was okay, I think," I answer uncertainly.

"You think? You spent the night with him! Was he good?"

"He was fine," I say, noncommittally.

She puts down her book and looks at me.

"Fine? What does that mean? Did you enjoy yourself?"

"Yes. Sort of?"

"It's all right." Tiffany says, in a reassuring tone. "It can take a while. The first time is never the best."

"Maybe it will be better without the sheet," I tell her.

She looks at me quizzically. "What sheet?"

"You know, with the hole in it."

She is staring at me. "We need to talk," she says.

"I can't," I tell her, "I have to study."

CHAPTER THIRTEEN

I sit back on my bed and think about Chaim's kinky *ketubah*. No touching him on the chest? Why not? What if I want to wrap my arms around him? Half way around him? However far they reach?

I close my eyes and drift into a fitful sleep, filled with dreams of beds and broadloom, shackles and brisket.

Tiffany wakes me up. "There's a delivery here for you. You need to sign for it."

I open the box, wondering what it is.

"It's a MacBook. Looks like one of the old white ones," Tiffany says.

"Of course." I roll my eyes. "Chaim!"

"I think they discontinued this model years ago. It seems clean, a few nicks and scratches. Why did he send it?"

"He wanted me to do some research. Guess he didn't know I have a new iPad."

I sit with my cup of coffee, power up the computer. The screensaver features flying dreidels. Holy Moses, there's already an e-mail from Chaim.

> From: Chaim Silver
> Subject: Your Almost New Computer
> Date: March 12 2013 13:15
> To: Anatevka Stein
>
> Dear Miss Stein,
>
> I hope that you will use this MacBook in good health. It's not new, but it's in good condition. It was a steal on eBay.
> I thought it might help with any online research on the provisions of our kinky *ketubah*. You can also email me with any questions. I'm on Skype right now if you'd like to video chat. Fair warning: I am not wearing pants.
>
> Chaim Silver
> CEO, Silver Bagels Technology Holdings Dot Com Limited Inc.

I hit reply.

> From: Anatevka Stein
> Subject: My Almost New Computer
> Date: March 12 2013 13:20
> To: Chaim Silver

Thanks for the computer. I'm touched by your thoughtfulness and will put it to good use. The missing caps lock key isn't a problem. I can work around it. Incidentally, there's some porn on this computer. And a picture of a man's... thing. Anyone I know?

Anatevka

Almost instantaneously there is a response.

From: Chaim Silver
Subject: Your Almost New Computer
Date: March 12 2013 13:23
To: Anatevka Stein

Sorry about the porn and the photo, they should have been deleted. I thought I owed it to you to test the computer before sending it in case, *G-d* forbid, it was defective. The web cam definitely works! Also, I have attached a finalized version of our proposed kinky *ketubah* that I hope is to your liking. Contact me with any questions.

Chaim Silver
CEO and Vice-President for Self-Pleasuring

Silver Bagels Technology Holdings Dot
Com Limited Inc.

From: Anatevka Stein
Subject: Your Almost New Computer
Date: March 12 2013 13:26
To: Chaim Silver

Thank you for the contracts. I need to do
more research. Are there any particular
keywords you would recommend I use?

Anatevka

From: Chaim Silver
Subject: Your Almost New Computer
Date: March 12 2013 13:29
To: Anatevka Stein

Best to start with something mild so as not
to be overwhelmed. Try "kosher anal
fisting."

Chaim Silver
CEO and Vice-President
Silver Bagels Technology Holdings Dot
Com Limited Inc.

Chaim is so patient and helpful, how can I resist
him?

CHAPTER FOURTEEN

I have tons of schoolwork to do, but I decide to take a break and do some online research on Chaim's favorite pastime. Flogging… whipping… caning…. *Oy vey!* Is he serious? I need clear my head and think. The only place I can do that is at Saks. I don't buy anything, but I feel refreshed.

Back at my desk, I'm about to resume work on my metaphor paper when I notice a message from Chaim.

> From: Chaim Silver
> Subject: RE Offer{EnlargeYour#Penis@]!
> Date: March 13 2013 17:11
> To: Anatevka Stein
>
> > Shocking Natural Penis Enlargement Secrets!
> > Add 2-4 Inches to YOUR Penis
> > The Answer Exposed
> > Right HERE

My *schwanz* is not big enough? And you would know this how, Anatevka, my previously *unshtupped* one? Never have I had a complaint about Little Chaim, I should live so long.

Chaim Silver
More-Than-Adequately-Endowed CEO and Vice-President
Silver Bagels Technology Holdings Dot Com Limited Inc.

What does this mean? He seems angry, but I have no idea what this is about.

When I glance up, there's Chaim! He's standing in the doorway of my bedroom, in his trademark dark suit, white shirt buttoned all the way up with no necktie, his silver yarmulke at a rakish angle, his *tzitzit* hanging just so. What is he doing here?

"I got your message," he says. "In fact, I got it twelve times. I think you made your point."

"I didn't send you that penis message. If it came from me, maybe that old computer you gave me has a virus."

"Oy vey." He looks stricken. "I'm sorry Anatevka, how could I have made such a mistake?"

"It's okay," I reassure him. "What were you going to do if I had sent it?"

"I would have given you such a spanking, your

tushy would burn like a chandelier. And that's just for starters."

Oh. Oooh. The effect is electric. My breath hitches. My stomach clenches. *Oy vey.* I am turned on by the idea!

In an instant, he is on top of me, groping me on the bed. The bedsprings complain loudly. My inner yenta complains loudly. I wonder if the neighbors will complain loudly.

I feel his body along the full length of mine, or at least along three-quarters of the length of mine. His tongue possesses me. Then dispossesses me. Then repossesses me and sells me at a discount. Holy Moses.

From inside his suit he pulls out a *tallit*, the white, fringed silk shawl that Jewish men wear to pray.

"*Tsatskeleh* I am going to tie you up like no one has ever tied you up before," he says.

"No one has ever tied up me before."

"Oh." He seems deflated. "In that case, then, like no one will ever tie you up in the future."

"Actually, I doubt anyone else will ever tie me up in the future."

"Don't be a wisenheimer," he says impatiently and begins knotting the prayer shawl.

Straddling me like a professional wrestler, he wraps the *tallit* around my wrists, tying it firmly. Then he knots the end to my headboard.

My inner yenta is calling 911.

"Trust me," he says.

Oy vey,

"Stand up," he orders.

"I can't," I protest. "I'm tied to the headboard and you're sitting on me."

"Ach, of course."

He begins to undress me slowly as I lie there, helpless. Layer by layer, my clothes come off, though when he reaches my shirt and bra, the *tallit* binding my arms prevents him from removing them completely. He can only pull them over my head.

"Omigod, I can't breathe," I pant.

"I know, *tsatskeleh*. I knew you would like this. Sexy, isn't it?"

"No," I gasp. "Air. Shirt. Help. Choking."

"*Oy*, sorry." He rearranges the fabric bunched around my head and neck.

Then he rolls me onto my stomach and places me across his knees.

"I will now spank you, my little *latke*," he announces.

Kinky, yet informative. My Chaim!

He places his hand on my naked behind, fondling me, stroking me, touching, groping, probing, squeezing. He's really enjoying himself. I await the first spank with eagerness mingled with dread. And wait. And wait.

"Um, Chaim, were you about to do something to me?"

"*Oy*, of course, the spanking," he exclaims, returning to himself.

The spanking commences. It stings, but it's not so bad. "I have to get something," he says. "Back in a moment."

I hear the clink of ice and feel ice cubes on my eager, yielding skin. Chaim rubs them over every part of me—my back, my nipples, my navel and... there! I tremble with each touch. My teeth are chattering. Must keep the circulation going. Who knew that freezer burn could be a sexually transmitted disease?

"You want I should fuck you, *tsatskeleh*?"

"Yes, please, Chaim, I want you should," I mewl.

Thank *G-d*. I need to warm up.

"Oh, Ana," he murmurs.

Thrusting, he thrusts into me with a thrust. I cry out. He takes me hard, plunging into me, pounding me, claiming me. I moan. He groans. I simper. He whimpers. He growls. I purr. He grunts. I gasp. He clenches his teeth. I clench my teeth. We clench each other's teeth. We reach a shattering climax and collapse, shattered. So this is sex!

I would hug Chaim, if only he would untie me. But I am still bound, and the knots in the *tallit* are now small and tight. He tries to loosen them but can't.

"Are you sure you've done this before?" I wonder aloud.

Chaim ignores me and continues to work at the knots, which only get tighter. This *tallit* idea is not working out very well. It would be so much simpler if Jewish men wore furry handcuffs to pray.

"*Tstatkseleh*, do you have a scissors?" he asks, finally.

"On the desk," I mumble.

A few minutes later, I am free and the silk shawl is in shreds.

I suggest to Chaim that he ask his Talmud instructor whether it's okay to use a *tallit* in a sexual act and then cut it into little pieces.

"Still the wisenheimer!" he says. "You want I should spank you again?"

As it is, I have deep red marks from the binding and a few scrapes from the scissors. I show Chaim my wrists.

"I'm sorry *tsatskeleh*, I'll make it up to you," Chaim says. "Brunch tomorrow?"

"Yes," I say. "But isn't Passover the next day?"

"Yes it is, my little Israelite slave girl, it's *Erev Pesach*," he says. "The perfect time to discuss our contract. Come by my place early. We'll talk about Jews in bondage."

"Oy vey," I say.

"Laters, *tsatskeleh,"* he says as he leaves.

CHAPTER FIFTEEN

Chaim is grasping a giant salami. It's long, shiny and massive—bigger than most salamis I've seen in stores. He is wearing his trademark dark suit, white shirt buttoned all the way up, no necktie. I am standing, naked, legs spread, wrists shackled to a Star of David.

He slaps the salami with his palm and grins at me. From behind, he places the salami under my nose.

"Big enough now?" he says. "Satisfied with your natural enlargement secrets?"

He runs the salami across my lips, which are parted and panting. My mouth and nostrils are filled with its salty, spicy aroma. He pulls it away, teasingly dragging the hard skin around my neck, across my breasts, down the small of my back. Then he slaps me with it. Hard, loud slaps.

Centuries of wandering, persecution and shtetl food are all packed into each salami-filled smack. Now he is touching me with the salami—there!—then hitting me, now touching me—there again! I explode in a breathtakingly intense orgasm rich in fat, sodium, nitrates, and kosher meat and meat by-products.

I wake up covered in perspiration. I don't even like salami.

What am I supposed to do today? Holy Moses, I'm supposed to meet Chaim for brunch and I've overslept! I shower and dress in haste. As always, I borrow some of Tiffany's clothes. Best. Roommate. Ever.

If I'm late, who knows what Chaim will do to me?

Schneider answers the door when I arrive and leads me to the kitchen.

Chaim is slouching at the breakfast table, a goblet of dark fluid in his hand. He's dressed as he was in my dream -- dark suit, white shirt buttoned all the way up, no necktie, and *tzitzit*. Around his yarmulke, his domed head gleams like a solar eclipse. He notices me, and rises to greet me.

"Tsatskeleh!" he says, in his unique, singsong whine. "Come in! Please! Sit. Boy, do you look hotsy-totsy!"

He's beaming as he pulls out a kitchen chair for me. "Join me for a drink."

He pours me a glass.

"This is very strong. What is it?" I ask.

Cherry cough syrup? Fermented prune juice? Chaim has such an adventurous palate. I have so much to learn.

"Slivovitz!" He beams. "Brandy. From plums. It's kosher for Pesach. What's not to like?"

He looks serious. "So you are considering the contract?"

"It would never stand up in court," I tell him. I don't know if that's true, but I heard someone say that on *The Good Wife*.

"Yes, so people say. Then they meet Levine, Levine & Levine. Believe you me, you don't want to mess with them. Particularly Levine."

"Well, unlike other people, I still have some issues."

"Talk to me, *tsatskeleh*. I'm a reasonable man."

"I don't want to eat kugel constantly. That's insane."

"Where does it say that?"

I show him.

"That's '*kegel* constantly.' It's an exercise."

"Whatever."

"So we'll skip that."

"I'm not sure about accepting free clothes. It feels wrong." I shift uncomfortably.

"Why not? It gives me pleasure to dress you, my *shayne maydl*."

"As long as you don't spend too much."

"You can count on that," he assures me. "What else?"

"No cutting. Nothing that would leave scars or marks."

"Ach, of course not. I hate the sight of blood. Why do you think I went into baking instead of medicine?"

"No threesomes. No swapping." I am firm on this. "I don't care if your rabbi himself commands you to share me."

"Fine," he says, his voice rising in pitch. "Though he'll be disappointed!"

"That thing with the sturgeon and the Vaseline and the car battery? I can't possibly agree to that."

"Of course not. Can't blame me for trying."

"And no tickling. I hate being tickled."

"If you say so. The submissive is always right."

"So it's a deal?" he s asks.

"No," I hesitate. "And then there's you. Why don't you like to be touched?"

"Because I'm fifty shades of *meshuggener*. I thought we were saving this for later."

I blink down at him. "Have you ever let anyone touch your chest? Caress you?"

"Yes, a long time ago. There was a woman. When I was in camp. The nurse. Mrs. Rosenberg. I went to the infirmary with a medical emergency and she seduced me. Did I have medical emergencies after that! *Oy vey*, so many injuries, every day, even before breakfast, all summer long. No one has touched me the same way since."

Seduced by an older woman as an adolescent! Poor Chaim. No wonder he's still single.

I'm angry and jealous! Why didn't I think of seducing an adolescent? Young, untainted, desperate to please. So much easier to manage than the college guys I meet. This is something to keep in mind down the road.

"So that's it?" he says. "We've addressed all your issues?"

I take a deep breath.

"Yes."

I nod shyly, and his black eyes widen.

"I had a dream last night," I tell him. "You were in it."

Picking up a kosher pickle, I gaze at him and bite my lip. Then very slowly, I put the tip of the pickle in my mouth and suck it.

"You don't say?" he says, his voice rising. "And what was I doing."

"You had a salami. A fat, long one. Naturally enlarged."

"*Tsatskeleh*, I like this dream. And what was I doing with this salami?"

"You were hitting me with it."

"Ooh! Go on."

"And touching me with it. Everywhere."

"Most interesting," he says, breathing a little irregularly. Chaim is trying to look nonchalant, but his eyes tell a different story.

"Are you hungry?"

"Not for food," I whisper.

Are those blue and orange flames shooting from his ears?

"Maybe I can offer you… something else that would be more to your liking?" he says to me, his voice rising again.

"I haven't actually signed anything yet."

"So, *nu,* let's skip the agreement for one more day. If there's a problem, Levine, Levine & Levine will sort it out. They have an excellent litigation department."

"Are you going to hurt me?"

"Yes, *tsatskeleh*, but I'll be hurting you for your own good. It will hurt me more than it hurts you."

"I'm so sorry. Please try not to hurt yourself too much."

We are standing, locked in an embrace. I should run, but I can't. He's wide, and he's blocking the door. Besides, I am mesmerized—like a moth drawn to flame, a bee to a hive, a magnetic note holder to an over-stocked, kosher refrigerator. The attraction is just too strong.

"How I want to tie you up and whip and slap you

until you scream," he muses, in his singsong whine. "*Oy*, such paradise that would be."

"Yes, that would be lovely," I purr.

"Come, my little *kichel*."

He takes my hand and we leave the kitchen together.

What have I just consented to? And is a *kichel* a dumpling or a pastry? I have got to learn these things.

My heart is pounding. My inner yenta is in the crash position, braced for impact. He opens the door and I am once more in the Blue Room of Broadloom.

CHAPTER SIXTEEN

It's the same as before, the menorah, the Star of David, the faint chemical smell of the clear vinyl slipcovers. On the stereo, an orchestra plays a mournful melody.

"'*Hatikvah*,'" Chaim answers, before I even ask.

My heart is pounding and my insides are rumbling like a column of Israeli tanks.

Chaim looks more animated than before, more rotund, and there's more swagger in his paunch.

"*Tsatskeleh*, when you're in here, you are mine," he says. "You will address me as '*Melech Ha* Bagel.'"

"What?" I answer.

"'King of the Bagels.' Never mind, just call me 'Your Bagelness.' You understand?"

"Yes."

"Yes, what?"

"Yes, Your Bagelness?"

"Very good. Undress and put these on," he orders softly, pointing to a screen in the corner behind which I am supposed to change.

"What are these, Your Bagelness?" I ask.

"Clothes. And a *mitpachat.*"

"*G-d* bless you. A what?"

"A *mitpachat.* A hair covering. You'll figure it out. And that's '*G-d* bless you, Your Bagelness.'"

I go behind the screen and do as I am told. These clothes are not very sexy. Thick black stockings, a long, matronly black skirt, and a long-sleeved pullover white shirt. The hair covering is a large pouch with a couple of ties to tighten it. There are even shoes to wear, heavy and black, with straps across the arches.

I feel utterly transformed. I emerge from behind the screen looking like an Orthodox housewife.

Chaim looks at me, wide-eyed.

"You are one hot BILF," he says admiringly.

"What?"

"*Balaboosta* I'd like to fuck. So, *nu,* how do you feel?" he asks.

"Hot," I tell him.

"I knew you'd like it."

"No, I mean I'm warm. This fabric is very heavy."

"From now on, in here, you'll wear these clothes. Now I'm going to take them off of you."

"Seriously? It was a lot of work to put all this gear on."

His expression changes. He seems angry.

"Yes, Your Bagelness," I quickly say.

Chaim beams. "You'll go places, *tsatskeleh*. Now, lift your arms up over your head."

He pulls my shirt up over my head and flings it aside, his breath and fingertips touching me as he does so. My breath hitches. Holy Moses. He unzips the skirt, and it drops onto the floor, where he leaves it. I can see what his mother means about him not being neat. He removes the head covering, letting my hair fall to my shoulders.

"Turn around."

I turn obediently. He starts to unclasp my bra, slowly, very slowly, agonizingly slowly. This is taking forever! The clasp is rubbing painfully against my skin and I feel his breath on my neck.

"Can I help?" I offer, quickly adding, "Your Bagelness."

"Tcha! Almost got it. *Oy*, it's so small, and what with the fingers and this tiny thing and you and the clothes and your hair in the way and…."

Finally, he stops whining and I feel my bra dropping onto the floor with the rest of my clothes. Then I feel the touch of his gentle, soft, stubby fingers. My nipples harden, my breath hitches. Blood surges through my veins like hot borscht. I moan.

"Turn around," he orders.

I obey.

"You smell amazing Anatevka," he whispers,

"Your scent is quite powerful too, Your Bagelness," I whisper back.

His aroma has so many levels! Today, it's onions and perspiration, with notes of herring. I must remember to go to Sephora and buy him some men's body wash.

"Give me your right hand."

I give him my hand. He turns it palm up, and before I know it, he swats the center with a hard salami that I hadn't noticed in his right hand. Where did that come from? What a magician!

It doesn't hurt, or at least not as much as I would have thought it would hurt to get hit with a premium salami.

"Nu, *tsatskeleh*?" he asks.

I blink at him, confused.

"It's time you should be shackled. You can still slide around the room, it shouldn't be a total loss."

I glance up at the network of metal bars. Its main branches resemble a menorah.

Oy vey.

"Put your hands up above your head."

He stands very close as he cuffs me. He takes off

his shirt. I notice he has a few faint small, round scars in a geometric pattern on his torso. Chicken pox? Some other childhood disease? Chaim is so complex, even his skin condition is an enigma. I wonder if I will get to meet his dermatologist in the sequel.

He traces a circle around my navel with the tip of the salami, teasing and tantalizing me. At the touch of the cold, hard roll, I quiver and inhale sharply.

"Beg me to touch your *pupik*," he instructs.

I'm confused but I obey.

"Please. Touch my *pupik*, Your Bagelness."

"Tell me that no one does it the way I do!"

"No one has ever touched my *pupik* with a salami the way you do, Your Bagelness," I manage to say.

It's no lie.

He traces a line around the middle of my body with the tip. Suddenly he flicks the salami against my behind... and then against my sex. I cry out in surprise. All my nerve endings stand at attention. I pull against the cuffs and shackles. I had no idea kosher cured meat could make this feel this way. I gasp.

He walks around me again and flicks the salami against me in the same place, again. *Oy vey.* My body convulses. I can't take much more.

My nerve endings are on fire as he hits one nipple, then the other. I cry out.

"So, *nu,* it's a pretty good salami, yes?" he breathes.

"Yes."

He hits me again with the salami, a stinging blow.

"Yes what?"

"Yes, Your Bagelness," I whimper.

Very slowly, he rains small, biting licks down my body. I know where this salami is headed. Still, nothing prepares me for the flood of sensation when it gets there. I am lost in a sea of savory, smoky salami-induced sensuality and I cry out.

"You are hungry for this, Ana, yes, my little kaiser roll? Open your mouth. Have a nosh, eat, enjoy."

He pushes the salami into my mouth, just like in my dream. My eyes are locked on his as my mouth closes around it. I can taste its salt and spice. *Oy vey!* So flavorful. Kosher salami is delicious!

He yanks it away grabs me and kisses me hard. His tongue invades me like it's Israel and my gums are Egypt in the 1967 War. Holy Moshe Dayan! How soon will he attack Jordan?

"You want I should I make you come?"

"Please," I beseech him.

The salami slams into my rear.

"Your Bagelness," I quickly add, my voice quavering.

"With this?" He holds the salami up. "Or maybe I should go get a carp?"

"Salami is good, Your Bagelness."

He nods, and proceeds with the skill of an artist in delicatessen meat. *Oy vey.* The onslaught is merciless.

He teases me, strokes me, and touches me—there—again and again. I can't take it anymore. I dissolve into a mouthwatering, perfectly cured Hebrew National orgasm. "Oh, Your Bagelness!" I shout.

My legs turn to jelly, but I'm still shackled. He grabs me and holds me up.

His arms curl around me. He lifts me and unzips his fly with one hand. Tethered to the ceiling, I lift my legs to wrap them around his belly and hips. They don't reach all the way around, but his love handles hold me in place.

Suddenly, he's deep inside me. This time, he's the Israeli air force and I'm Saddam Hussein's Osirak reactor. I'm crumbling in gigantic explosions as he thrusts again and again, wheezing and gulping, his eyes bulging his cheeks reddening, the veins in his neck swelling. Will he be a casualty of this raid? Is it *kaddish* for Chaim? I lose all self-control, writhing with uncontainable ecstasy.

He has completely stopped moving. He is groaning and gritting his teeth.

"Chaim? Are you okay?"

"My back," he grunts.

"Are you hurt?"

"*Oy*, just a spasm. Nothing serious, but I need to lie down."

"Can you move?"

"Not exactly."

This is not good. My legs are rubber and I'm completely drained.

"Can you unshackle me?"

Grimacing, bent like a hunchback, he manages to raise his arms and unshackle one of my wrists, and I do the other.

"Your Bagelness?"

"Bed," he says. "I need to lie flat for a few minutes. I'll live."

I find my clothes and put on enough of them to be decent in case Schneider or Chaim's mother are wandering around. There's an old, stained terry cloth robe hanging on the door and I drape it over Chaim. Then I lead him to his bedroom, supporting his arms, as he takes short, shuffling steps, muttering "*Oy, oy, oy*" with each one.

He rolls onto the bed and lies on his side, in an almost fetal position. I find his heating pad, plug it in, and place it against his back. Then I crawl into bed beside him.

Kosher sex is exhausting! My last thoughts are "My Chaim!" before I fall into a deep sleep.

CHAPTER SEVENTEEN

I'm hanging by a silk tallit from the ceiling of a delicatessen. Around me are assorted salamis, a glass case filled with smoked fish, chopped liver, and barrels of pickles. Chaim is examining me. "This one looks geshmak," *he says, and pinches my waist. "Do you have a scissors?" Holding my waist, he snips the tallit and I fall to the floor.*

"Wake up!" he says. Chaim is standing over me, pinching me gently. "We have to leave in half an hour. My parents are making a Seder."

Oh. I've been dreaming again. Chaim looks better. Though he's a little stiff and he reeks of Ben Gay.

I get up and limp into the bathroom. I am drained, inside and out. No wonder he wants me to kegel constantly! I shower and dry myself quickly and look for my clothes. I should say Tiffany's clothes.

They're in a mound on the floor where Chaim has thoughtfully tossed them.

"My *bubbe* and *zeyde* will be there," he informs me.

I really need to look my best.

I put my slip on. I shake out Tiffany's little red dress and put it on. It's a clingy number that stops at the top of my thighs. It's almost a shirt. I'm wearing it with killer high heels. I check myself in the mirror. Slutty dress? Check. Porn star shoes? Check. Bedroom hair? Check. Hickies, freshly fucked complexion? Check. Too much red lipstick? Check. I'm ready for this. I hug myself, knowing I'm going to make a great impression.

And yet, something is gnawing at me. The look doesn't feel quite complete. What is wrong?

Chaim has left a tumbler of dark fluid for me on the bureau. He thinks of everything! I really am dehydrated and could go for some cranberry juice and club soda. I take a sip and it's Coca-Cola. But no Coke I have ever had has tasted so sweet. It's really, really sweet. All this sex has enhanced my taste buds.

I enter the living room, fizzy drink in hand.

Chaim sees me and smiles. "You like? It's Kosher for Passover. Made with sugar, not corn syrup. Pretty good, *nu*?"

He's already dressed in one of his twenty identical outfits of dark suit and white shirt. "Lay Lady Lay" is playing on the stereo.

"I didn't figure you for a Bob Dylan fan," I say.

"Robert Alan Zimmerman," Chaim counters. "Nice Jewish boy from Minnesota."

He takes my hands and we dance slowly, as the lyrics waft through the room.

Lay, lady, lay, lay across my big brass bed.

"You're not a bad lay yourself, lady!" Chaim says with a smirk.

He says the sweetest things.

"Where did you learn to dance?" I ask him.

"From Mrs. Rosenberg," he explains. "It was part of my treatment."

"The fox-trot was part of your treatment?"

That woman!

No answer. He seems lost in the music. Is he thinking of me —or her?

Abruptly, we have to leave.

"We're going to be late," Chaim says, anxiously. "My mother will kill me."

He grabs my hand and rushes me toward the door. Oh, the many moods of Chaim Silver. Will I ever be able to understand this irresistible, impetuous mensch?

"Okay, okay," I tell him.

I grab my handbag, though I'm still sure I'm forgetting something. What is it? Just as he opens the door to leave, I realize what it is.

"Wait, my panties!" I exclaim.

Chaim sighs impatiently.

Quickly, I slip them off and hand them to him. Now my look is complete. What was I thinking, leaving the house with those still on? He nods and puts them in his pocket.

CHAPTER EIGHTEEN

We walk down one flight of stairs to the apartment below.

Mrs. Silver is at the front door waiting for us. Her dress is a shiny aquamarine that contrasts nicely with her orange chair. Beyond her, seated in a deep reclining chair, is Mr. Silver, short, rotund, his bald head sporting a few gray hairs. I can see Chaim's features in his.

She says something very sternly to Chaim in Yiddish.

"Mama, we just came from upstairs!" he protests.

"We forgot to wipe our feet," he whispers to me.

"Ana, this is my Father."

I smile at Mr. Silver.

"Please don't get up," I say, and he doesn't. "It's very nice to meet you."

Mr. Silver grunts his acknowledgment. He and Chaim are cut from the same cloth.

Mrs. Silver takes my hand.

"So nice to see you again," she says. I feel myself blushing all over.

"Are they here yet?"

I hear a loud, impatient voice from within.

"That would be Mischa, my sister," he says.

She comes out of the kitchen, large and orange haired like her mother. Chaim's sister is in her mid-to-late forties. She does not seem happy to see us.

I try to smile. Mischa is taking me in from head to toe, very slowly.

"So you're Chaim's latest friend? " says Mischa. "I'll bet you're something special."

"Thanks!" I reply. I really hope I can live up to her expectations.

The living room is spacious, simply furnished in brown, olive green, and beige, with a few colorful throw pillows. Seated and standing are members of the Silver's extended family—his bubbe and zeyde, aunts and uncles, in-laws, nieces and nephews. There are about twenty of them.

"We're going to start soon, Ana," Mrs. Silver says. "A few more minutes."

Maybe we're waiting for more relatives, or sundown. I sit and cross my legs. All the men in the

Silver family are looking at me. How nice of them to take such so much interest!

"So," Mr. Silver says.

But then he says nothing. Mischa jumps in.

"Where did you two meet?"

"I interviewed Chaim for the Baruch Hillel Newsletter."

I hope that passes muster.

Mr. Silver grunts.

"And your plans after school?" she asks.

"Publishing, I think. I have an interview with a publishing company specializing in sex education books for Jewish children. Maybe you've seen *Everyone Shtups?* I have an interview soon. I'm going to take a few days off first. Maybe visit my Mom in New Jersey."

Mr. Silver grunts again.

Chaim looks surprised.

"You're going away?"

"Englewood isn't exactly 'away.' People commute from there every day."

"You'll go alone? There are maniacs out there, you know," he says. "*Oy vey.* When do you depart?"

Depart for New Jersey? Like I need a boarding pass? Hello?

"I'll go after graduation, I suppose. No big deal. Hang out with my Mom, do some shopping at the mall, sleep."

Chaim is not soothed.

"Have you been to Israel?" Mischa interjects.

Her tone makes me nervous. I know she will not like my answer.

"No, but I'd love to go."

She grimaces and nods.

"Mischa runs birthright tours." Mrs. Silver says proudly. "Teenagers get a free trip to Israel to discover their roots. All expenses paid by Jewish organizations. Hers are the best —completely kosher. She's very strict."

"Israel is beautiful," Mischa says. "You have to go. I'll tell you exactly where to stay and what to do."

Maybe Chaim's dominant tendencies are genetic.

"I think Ana would like London," Chaim says softly.

He remembers my chick-lit preferences. So sweet!

"The Tower of London. And all those castles with dungeons."

Wait, those would be his preferences.

The Seder begins. They read quickly from the Haggadah, in Hebrew, but they're not leaving out a single thing. This is going to take forever! When we finally reach the Four Questions, it falls to Chaim's nephew, Shmuel, to chant them. He's the youngest male at the table.

Mah nishtanah, ha-laylah ha-zeh, mi-kol ha-leylot?

I don't speak Hebrew, but I know what he's saying. "Why is this night different from all other nights?"

As he recites, Chaim places his hand on my thigh and squeezes gently. My breath hitches. *Oy vey...* so that's why this night is going to be different.

She-b'khol ha-leylot 'anu 'okhlin chameytz u-matzah, ha-laylah ha-zeh, kulo matzah?

That must be the question about why we eat matzah. Hmm…. An interesting question, but I'm more focused on other questions. How long can I hold on?

I feel Chaim's warm hands near my sex and I'm keenly reminded that I'm not wearing underwear. I bite my lip.

She-b'khol ha-leylot 'anu 'okhlin sh'ar y'raqot, ha-laylah ha-zeh, maror?

Why do we eat bitter herbs? The better to climax by, maybe? *Oy.* I feel a clenching in my stomach. I think I know the answer to all four questions: "Yes, yes, yes, yes!"

> *She-b'khol ha-leylot 'eyn 'anu matbilin 'afilu pa`am 'achat, ha-laylah ha-zeh, shtey fe`amim?*

I know this one too. It's about how, on all other nights, we don't dip our food even once, yet on this night we dip twice. Speaking of dipping, Chaim is touching me... there... and I'm gripping the table edge. I think, "Please stop!" but my inner yenta is shouting, "Happy Passover!"

Fortunately the kid has asked four questions. I couldn't have lasted one more second.

But then he continues:

> *She-b'khol ha-leylot 'anu 'okhlin beyn yoshvin u-veyn m'subin, ha-laylah ha-zeh, kulanu m'subin?*

WTF? It's the question about why on this night we eat reclining. Not to be technical, but isn't that five questions? Jewish prayers and Jewish men. So hard to figure out! I clamp my legs shut like a bear trap and remove Chaim's hand. Disaster averted.

Mischa looks at the two of us sternly. She is not amused.

At 10PM, we're half way through the Seder, so finally we get to eat. Mrs. Silver insists I try her homemade gefilte fish.

"I'm really not hungry," I tell her.

"So?" she says.

I guess everyone in this family is a sadist.

We feast on *matzah* balls, brisket, *matzah* farfel, carrot and sweet potato *tzimmes*, fried potato *latkes*, and gravy. *Oy vey!*

The dinner table talk turns to casual conversation and family gossip. Mischa recounts her adventures in Israel, lapsing into fluent Hebrew. We stare at her, and she stares back, puzzled, until Chaim tells her what she's doing. How we all laugh! Then Chaim's hard-of-hearing Uncle Sidney starts talking over her about his own recent adventures. I had no idea how interesting laparoscopic gall bladder surgery could be.

I sigh and peek at Chaim. I could stare at him forever, his shiny skin, his pink jowls and deep frown lines. He pulls at my chin with his soft, damp fingers. So tender! Is this a PDA? Or was I dribbling gravy? Who knows? Will I ever truly understand this complex, mysterious yid? Will this Seder ever end?

CHAPTER NINETEEN

The children are excused from the table to hunt for the hidden *affikoman*, a piece of *matzah* that is traditionally the object of a treasure hunt. The Seder can't resume until it is found, and the lucky kid who finds it usually gets a "ransom" or prize. Chaim takes my hand and leads me from the table with them.

"So, *tsatskeleh*. Perhaps I should give you a tour of the rest of the house?" he asks in his lilting whine.

I don't know what this means, but I'm worried.

He leads me through the kitchen while the Seder guests are distracted by the activity of the children. We go downstairs into a musty storage area. There's a lawnmower, gardening tools, buckets, and household cleaning products. It smells of mold and ammonia.

"*Tsatskeleh*, honey, my little *matzah brei*, I'm going to spank you and then fuck you," he says beaming.

"I don't want to be spanked here," I plead with him.

Next to me are several plastic jugs labeled "weed killer."

"How about between the power washer and the leaf blower?"

"Mmm... I don't think so."

"Okay, *tsatskeleh*. In that case we'll just *shtup*. But don't come. I want we should finish with you aching and frustrated. Won't that be more fun?"

My Chaim! He always has such good suggestions. I would never have thought of it.

I caress his cheek, running my fingers across his shiny bare scalp. It's smooth and wet. He moans and his breathing falters.

"Why wouldn't you let me finger you at the dinner table, with my family present and my nephew reciting the Four Questions?"

So that's why he wanted to spank me next to the weed blower or the leaf washer or whatever! Yes, I was being a bit inconsiderate, I suppose.

"Sorry. I'm always thinking of myself. I should have been more unselfish. Maybe at the next holiday?"

"It's a date, *tsatskeleh*. Simchat Torah, at services. Now brace yourself. This is going to be brief—my back is still giving me a pain."

With one push, he's inside me. He groans. Is it from pleasure or indigestion? Who can have sex after a meal like that?

"Ana!" he cries.

"I know," I commiserate, "your Mother's *matzah* balls are so heavy, like a—"

But before I can say "lead weight" or "Napoleonic-era cannon ball," he finds his release.

There are footsteps upstairs.

"Chaim!" Mischa shouts.

Oy vey. We rearrange ourselves in a hurry.

"Coming, Mischa," Chaim calls to her. "I still want to spank you," he whispers to me.

We hear louder footsteps, then the door opens.

"We're about to start again," Mischa says. She looks with suspicion first to Chaim, then to me. "What are you two doing in here?"

"We were, um, looking for the *affikoman*," Chaim tells her. He doesn't sound very convincing. "It's not down here."

"Yes, of course you were. The kids found it fifteen minutes ago. You know it's always in the couch cushions. Hurry up, everyone's waiting."

She shakes her head and leaves.

I wonder if she suspects something.

Two hours later, the Seder concluded, we say our goodbyes.

Chaim's mother hands me a small package that weighs a ton.

"A little Passover cake for Chaim's coffee. A secret recipe."

Instead of flour, *matzah* and a touch of Portland Cement, I feel sure.

She hugs me. I turn to her husband.

"Mr. Silver, good-bye and thank you."

He grunts.

As we make our exit, Mischa glares at me. And then we are on the flight of stairs to Chaim's apartment.

The journey home gives me time to think. With each step up the staircase, Chaim has come into sharper focus. He is no savior, just a man, emotionally flawed, overweight, dragging me into a world that is dark, mysterious, and high in fat and calories.

When we reach his front door less than a minute later, it feels like we have journeyed far together. His apartment is in shadows. Chaim always turns off all the table lamps and overhead lights when he goes out. "I should have to support Con Edison?" he often asks. And yet, the dark living room still has an eerie, pale glow. Just like Chaim!

"Thank *G-d*. We made it," Chaim murmurs, flipping on the light switch.

"Yes. Yes we have."

Somehow he and I, together, have managed to climb our way through the darkness. We couldn't have done it without each other, or the one small LED Muppet nightlight he left plugged into an electrical outlet.

"Tired Miss Stein?"

"Yes, Mr. Silver."

I nuzzle him, but he pulls back. I realize I almost put my hands on his chest. His big hard limit!

"Why can't I touch you? Tell me please?" I ask.

"We've discussed this. Not yet."

"How about a deal? I let you do something weird to me that I will probably enjoy anyway. In exchange, you tell me a private detail about yourself that sheds very little light on anything, so people still have to keep reading if they want answers."

"It's a deal, *tsatskeleh*. You know how to *hondle!* So, first, my turn," Chaim says. "Stand in front of me."

I do as I'm told.

"Arms at your sides," he orders.

He unzips the back of my dress. Then grasps the hem. With one swift, magical motion, he yanks it down. He nearly yanks me to the floor with it. There's a loud ripping sound as my dress loosens and falls to the floor. I should say Tiffany's dress. So funny! How she will laugh when she finds out.

Chaim kisses me softly and caresses my naked body with his soft, moist hands.

"I've missed this," Chaim says, in a voice tinged with nostalgia and regret. "How long has it been?"

"A couple of hours?"

"Ahh," he sighs.

He goes over to the bureau and returns with a handful of items. New toys? *Oy vey.* What have I agreed to?

He hands me a set of shiny chrome balls, connected by a thread. They're almost spherical but not quite. They seem lumpy and parts of the polished surface are a bit dull and pockmarked.

"Ben Wa *matzah* balls."

"Ben Who?" I ask.

"Ben Wa balls, *tsatskeleh*. Kosher for Passover. Completely metal. They look just like *matzah* balls, but they go inside you."

Oy vey!

"Are the balls clean?"

"Yes, I got a fresh new set."

"Are you sure you don't need a bigger pair?"

"No, the salesman assured me that I had a pair that would clank."

My Chaim!

He fingers me until I am as soft and slippery as the coating on his mother's gefilte fish. Then he inserts the Ben Wa *matzah* balls one by one inside me.

"Tsatskeleh dear, go get me some Manischewitz."

I do as I'm told. I know he just wants me to feel the Ben Wa *matzah* balls inside me as I move, and I do. They rattle around like coins in a washing machine. *Oy vey.* I don't know whether to orgasm or call Sears.

He takes the cup of wine.

"Shall we resume the Seder?" Chaim asks. "'Blessed art Thou, Lord our *G-d*, Ruler of the Universe, Who created this *tuches*.' Now bend over. I'm going to spank you, it shouldn't be a total loss."

He brings his hand down on my butt over and over like he's Moses and my tushy is an evil Egyptian taskmaster. Though he also caresses me gently between blows, unlike Moses, until I am very aroused. If Moses had done it like this, the story of Passover would have ended very differently!

Gently, he teases each Ben Wa *matzah* ball out of me, pulling on the thread. As each one pops out, I almost climax. I'm so close.

"Say it, *tsatskeleh*," he orders. "Say it."

I can't believe he's making me beg and plead. But I can't take much more. So finally I do.

I shout at the top of my lungs, "Let my people come!"

Then he places his rod of Moses is inside me, parting my Red Sea wide open.

"Oh, *tsatskeleh*," he whispers.

An orgasm floods over both of us, just like the Red Sea washing over Pharoah's Army, but with more sex and less drowning.

"Happy Passover," Chaim murmurs, and we collapse.

CHAPTER TWENTY

We lie together in silence for a while.

"We had a deal, you know," I remind him.

"Don't be a *noodge*."

"I won't, if you start talking"

"We agree that this information will shed very little light on anything?"

"Yes."

"And that it will barely advance the plot?"

"Agreed."

"O.K. I had a rough start in life. Some bad stuff you don't need to know about."

"How bad?"

Poor Chaim.

"Well then, here it is: I was a teenage bed wetter."

Oh no. Not really.

"What a terrible secret to live with!"

"It wasn't a secret. At summer camp, everyone found out. That's when the wedgies began. Atomic wedgies, side wedgies, hanging wedgies, the Melvin."

They gave him a Melvin? No wonder he is driven to dominate the bagel industry. No wonder he can give love but can't receive. No wonder there is a rubber mattress cover on his bed. Poor Chaim. Tragic, ill-fated Chaim. Damp Chaim.

I'm quiet for a moment.

"A shekel for your thoughts?" he says.

"I still want more," I whisper.

"*Tsatskeleh*, baby, Little Chaim is really tired. I just don't know...."

"No, not more sex! Less sex. I want more of you, Chaim. To understand you, to love you, to be with you."

"*Oy*. I told you, girlfriends aren't my thing."

"Can't we compromise?"

"For example."

"You give up all your exotic, kinky interests, your dalliances with submissives, your sex toys, your Blue Room of Broadloom, and you become a monogamous, doting, puppyish boyfriend. In exchange, I'll let you take care of me financially."

"Hmm.... That *is* a very tempting offer, Miss Stein," he says.

"Thank you, Mr. Silver."

"You drive a hard bargain. For you, Anatevka, I will try."

I know he means it. My Chaim!

CHAPTER TWENTY-ONE

The auditorium is packed as Tiffany delivers her valedictory address. She is so awesome. I'm beaming as she speaks the words I heard her rehearsing so many times in her room.

> ...which is why we are special. We *can* have it all. That's one of the many lessons I've learned while going to school here at Baruch. I've learned that you can be skinny—and eat as much as you want. For this, I thank my fabulous metabolism and my personal trainer, Jorge. You can be rich, while investing only in socially responsible companies, as I've been doing with my trust fund since I turned 21. You can be in style and also be environmentally conscious with sustainable clothing, as typified by my own line of hemp beach sarongs, making their debut at Fashion Week this year. That's why I believe in

our generation. We are the future.
Especially me.

It's so inspiring I want to cry. In fact I do cry. I
also shout, "You rock, Tiffany!" and give her a solo
standing ovation.

The rest of the audience is a little more subdued.
They are still taking in her words.

Tiffany concludes her speech with a bow. Then
the Dean rises and introduces Chaim. Holy Moses,
Chaim's going to give a speech. I had no idea. The
Dean touches briefly on Chaim's achievements: Bagel
maven, CEO, self-made mensch. They're giving him
an honorary degree! People are pointing and saying,
"Just look at him!" and "Oh my *G-d*."

I'm bursting with pride. If they only knew.

Please welcome Mr. Chaim Silver.

The Dean shakes Chaim's hand, and there is polite
applause.   My heart is in my throat.   Chaim
approaches the lectern, which is taller than he is. Yet
he emerges above it.   He must be standing on
something.   Then he lowers the microphone and
surveys the hall:

> Such a great compliment you've paid me
> here today. I'm so grateful. More than
> that. I'm proud. When I gave my first

donation to the baking science department here at Baruch, I thought, "Well, it couldn't hurt." But you've done so much. Who knew?

In my family, I always had enough to eat, thank G-d. More than enough. My Mama, bless her, she would say, "Finish your dinner, there are people starving in Africa." My *bubbe* had said the same thing to her when she was a girl.

So we ate and ate all the time, even when we weren't hungry, thinking of those poor, hungry people. I would say to myself at every meal, "*Oy,* those poor starving Africans!"

Then I would have another *kreplach*, it shouldn't go to waste.

Then I realized I could do something to help. Throughout Africa there is political, ecological and social dysfunction. Where there is political, ecological and social dysfunction, there are no bagels. And without bagels, what is breakfast? So the people, they start the day grouchy and ready to hack their neighbors to pieces. Believe me, I've been there. And so, the cycle of poverty and starvation repeats itself, *nokh a mol.*

How can over a billion people, mainly in Sub-Saharan Africa, South Asia, and Latin

America live without any sort of bagel shop or delicatessen? A *shanda* and a *harpa* —a scandal and an outrage. So this is why I have been trying to develop viable and ecologically sustainable methods of providing bagels to third world countries. We distribute as many as we can to the areas in greatest need.

But, G-d willing, they should learn to make their own bagels and be self-sufficient. That's our goal. As the saying goes, "Give a man a bagel and he'll eat for a day. Teach him to make his own bagels from scratch and he'll say, 'That's a lot of trouble. Can't I have just one?'" But in the end, he'll be better off.

Now I remember the brief snippet of phone conversation I overheard about Darfur. It all falls into place. Problems with rugelach. Bagel and cream cheese deliveries. He was shipping them the breakfast and brunch ingredients they needed! It wasn't for profit. It was for peace.

The people of these *farkakteh* countries sometimes eat dirt. Believe me, I know what it's like to eat dirt. *Oy vey* do I know! We Jews have a word for that. We call it *schmutz*. And no one should ever have to eat it. I've made bagels in a lot of flavors, but I've never made a *shmutz* bagel. Who would buy that? A schmuck, that's who. So this is a very personal journey for me.

Chaim knows what it's like to eat *schmutz*? Yes of course he does. When he wet his bed in camp, bullies probably made him do that. I see young Chaim, a lost chubby boy, moist and chafing, on the ground in front of a group of bullies. My Chaim. My poor, *meshuggener* Chaim. My poor, *meshuggener*, kinky, overweight, philanthropic, bed-wetting, *schmutz*-eating Chaim.

If only a starving family in Ethiopia could order a deli sandwich—to go! Well, soon they will be able to. With our new stand-alone solar and hydro-electric powered bagel and rye-bread huts, families in Africa will be able to *fress* on corned beef in the most remote, impoverished villages. We're training whole villages of African children in the art of preparing Jewish food—slicing, dicing, under-seasoning, overcooking. It brings me so much *naches*, believe you me. We have it in our power to make everyone as fat and happy as my family. Today, I know that I am closer than ever to achieving my dream.

Chaim concludes his speech as the crowd roars its approval.

"That was a great speech," I tell him afterward.

"Thanks, *tsatskeleh*," he says. "You looked so sexy getting that diploma in your cap and gown"

Only Chaim and I know that I have nothing on underneath.

"I'm beginning to understand you," I tell him, gazing into his soulful black eyes.

We are at a reception, hosted by the dean. I am sipping sherry as Chaim pinches my ass.

"Come," he murmurs and leads me away from the crowd. He directs me to a window overlooking the sidewalk. Chaim is pointing, but an old, dented silver Hyundai Hatchback blocks our view.

"So?" I say. "I can't see anything. Some shitbox car is in the way."

"It's for you. Happy Graduation," he murmurs, pulling me into his arms, kissing my hair, and getting it caught in his teeth.

He bought me a car? *Oy.* I shake my head.

"It's a gift, Anatevka," he says. He spits out a strand of hair. "Can't you just accept it and say thank you?"

Am I ready for this level of commitment? Does accepting a car make me beholden to him? Well, no, not that car. It looks like it was hit by a rockslide.

"I'm not sure I can accept it. You really shouldn't have. Seriously. You shouldn't have."

I look at the car again. It's parked in a "No Standing Anytime" spot. An official New York City tow-truck has pulled up alongside it and the crew is attaching something.

Chaim isn't paying attention. "Anything for my little *tsatskeleh*," he says, beaming at me.

CHAPTER TWENTY-TWO

I arrive at the bus station an hour early at Chaim's request to ensure that I wouldn't miss the bus, less than the three hours he had insisted upon. We had argued and compromised. I text Chaim to let him know I'm here.

> Arrived at bus station. Departure any hour now. Itinerary includes nap in bedroom, trip to mall. Will send postcards.

He replies instantly:

> *Tsatskeleh*, don't be a wisenheimer. Be careful! It's not safe to travel alone. So many perverts take the bus, particularly that one. Believe me, I know! Why didn't you drive the Hyundai? I should spank your tushy for this.

I text back:

> Still impounded. No time to get to the lot they towed it to.

My tushy needs a vacation as much as I do.

The bus to Englewood makes good time across the George Washington Bridge. My Mom meets me at the bus stop and drives me home. I'm tired when we get there. I go to my room and sit on my pink bed surrounded by pink furniture. I hug my stuffed bear, Mr. Pinkerton. His soft, furry belly reminds me of Chaim and I start to cry.

"Anatevka," my Mom says. She has a deep, raspy voice from years of chain-smoking. She's puffing a cigarette. "I'm worried about your mood. You seem depressed."

My Mom is a therapist. She really understands people. I have her to thank for turning out the way I have.

"I had a long talk with your roommate. She says you're out all night, and when you return her clothes after borrowing them, she has to burn them. I'm concerned."

Oy vey.

"His name's Chaim. He's older. He makes bagels. He's complex and fascinating. Though he's always spanking me."

"Does he make you happy?"

My Mom has been married nine times. She knows stuff, especially about community property in the state of New Jersey. But I wonder if she will understand Chaim.

"He has some baggage. A bad experience in summer camp. Makes it hard for him to open up."

"Maybe he has other ways of expressing himself. What does he say?"

"Hmm…. That I'm hotsy-totsy. That I throw a pretty good *shtup*. That he can't wait to spank and fuck me. I think he wants to chain me to a rack shaped like a Star of David, attach clamps to my nipples, and have anal sex."

"Ana, this is wonderful! I'm so happy for you."

"Really?"

"Yes, sweetie. Follow your libido. You need to see where it leads."

My Mom lights up another cigarette and takes a long drag.

"My second husband liked me to put him in giant diapers and read him children's stories. *Goodnight Moon* really got him going. Husband number four couldn't come unless he was wearing my underwear. He was always stretching it out of shape. Your own father insisted I squeal like a dolphin. One night, he made me pretend I was caught in a tuna net. Ana, sweetie, that was the night you were conceived."

"Oh, Mom. Maybe Chaim does love me!"

I hug myself. I hug Mr. Pinkerton. My inner yenta hugs me. Then I hug my Mom. Then she hugs Mr. Pinkerton. Then I take a nap.

When I wake up, I feel better and I e-mail Chaim.

> From: Anatevka Stein
> Subject: Englewood Ho!
> Date: June 6 2013 18:15
> To: Chaim Silver
>
> I'm not sure that subject line looks right.
> Anywho, arrived safely. Miss you.
> Spending time with Mom and Mr.
> Pinkerton. He's a stuffed bear. Hope you
> are enjoying yourself alone. No, not that
> way.
>
> Your Ana

> From: Chaim Silver
> Subject: Englewood Ho!
> To: Anatevka Stein
> Date: June 6 2013 18:20
>
> Miss you too. Don't worry about me,
> alone with all my toys and no one to play
> with. You should enjoy yourself. I'll be
> fine. It's okay. I'm going to play the

accordion now. I have the sheet music to "All By Myself."

Chaim Silver
CEO, Silver Bagels Holdings Dot Com
Limited Inc.

P.S. I'm having dinner with an old friend tonight, it shouldn't be a total loss. Be kind to your mother.

P.P.S. Laters, *tsatskeleh*.

Old friend? Does Chaim have friends? I wonder if it's Mrs. Rosenberg! Perhaps one of his old summer camp "injuries" was bothering him again? *Oy vey.*

CHAPTER TWENTY-THREE

The following day is devoted to shopping. Afterward, my Mom and I have a celebratory girls night out at a nearby hotel bar. We sip cosmopolitans as she reminisces. By the fifth drink, she's on her fifth husband.

"He was sexually aroused only by furniture. He left me for a Hepplewhite sideboard."

The things she has been through! Chaim is seeming less and less strange the more I talk to her. What a great Mom. But there is still something off about him. I try to explain it to her.

"He's so possessive. No matter where I am or what I do, I always feel he's looking over my shoulder."

My mother seems distracted as I speak. She's looking right past me. When I turn my head, I see Chaim, right behind me. *Oy vey.*

He's here? Holy Moses! I'm speechless at first. Finally, I manage a greeting.

"Hello Chaim. This IS a surprise. Chaim, this is my mother. Mom, Chaim Silver."

"A pleasure, Mrs. Stein."

"So nice to meet you Mr. Silver. What a wonderful surprise. Please, call me Shirley."

"*Enchanté*, Shirley," he says bowing, and my Mother bats her eyelashes, smitten.

I feel my face flushing red. So suave, my Chaim.

"What brings you to New Jersey, Mr. Silver?"

"I needed to get away from the city for a little while," Chaim answers. "My doctor tells me I need to relax, go to the country, breathe some fresh air. I should argue?"

"You came here for fresh air?" I ask.

We're just off Route 4, and we can hear trucks.

"Where are you staying?" my mother asks cheerfully.

"I found a lovely place nearby," Chaim says. "The Hampton Inn. Looks homey."

"You do know there are, like, hundreds of them, everywhere," I point out.

"Really!" Chaim says. "Who knew? They say travel broadens the mind."

"Please, join us," my mother says and Chaim takes a seat. Chaim signals the waiter to come over.

"Peach schnapps for me, two cherries, dirty. And another round for the ladies," he offers.

"The inn is just down the road. I thought I would stop in here for a drink. Who knew I would find the two of you?"

He takes $10 out of his wallet. To pay for the drinks? I shake my head and he takes out a couple of twenties. I nod.

"Ana tells me you're in bagels," my Mom says, beaming at him.

Chaim places a soft, moist hand on mine. "Yes, you could say that. I'm in a lot of things. Babkas, rugelach, you name it. Everything I touch is warm, fresh and delicious." He squeezes my hand. I flush.

"Chaim has a factory," I volunteer.

"Why that's wonderful! That reminds me of my sixth husband. He had a factory. Hundreds of employees. Made pianos. Always insisting that I get on top of a piano and take off my—"

"Mom!"

I make frantic sawing gestures across my throat until she stops.

"Actually, if you two can excuse me for a moment, I need to go to the ladies room. I'll be right back!"

When she's gone, I glare at Chaim.

"I can't believe you followed me here!" I tell him.

115

At the same time, I'm flattered that he cared enough to stalk me.

"I was worried about you. Traveling alone. Taking buses. It's a dangerous world."

"We're in Englewood."

"Your mother is a very attractive woman," he says.

Did he just lick his lips?

"Yes, she is."

"I see a little of her in you. And you in her. The two of you are a very hot pair."

Where is he going with this?

"Chaim!"

"Oh, I know, it's expressly forbidden. Leviticus 18. It's hard to be a Jew! But a man can dream."

He is so crazy, my Chaim.

I decide to confront my worst fears.

"About your dinner with your 'old friend.' Was it... Her?"

"Yes, Ana... it was Her. Don't be such a *noodge*. She's just a friend. A business partner too."

"She's your partner?"

"She had *ein bissel* foot fetish, so I set her up in a Laser Toe-Nail Fungus Removal franchise. We get together every now and then and talk toes."

Holy Moses! Chaim might be stranger than

husband number five after all. What am I going to do?

When my mother returns, Chaim gets up to leave.

"So wonderful to meet you Mrs. Stei—Shirley. You have a lovely daughter. I'd love to chat some more but such a long day I've had, I think I need to head back to the Inn."

"Watch out for the traffic!" I warn him.

"Laters, *tsatskeleh*," he says with a wink and is gone.

My mother looks at me.

"Now THAT is a *ganser macher*."

"A what?"

She's annoyed with me.

"Listen sweetie, you have to kiss a lot of frogs in life to find the right frog. Believe me, I've smooched my share of them."

"So you think Chaim is the frog for me?"

"Let's just say a frog like that is worth trying to hold onto. You have to go to him. Now."

"Seriously? But I came home to see you."

"The man tracked you all the way to New Jersey to shadow you and sexually degrade you. This could be an important new stage in your relationship."

"Really?"

She's has been married to nine different men. And

she has a master's degree. Who am I to question her expert judgment?

"Everything you need to be happy is at the Hampton Inn. And I don't mean the free donuts in the morning."

Oh Mom! I can see tears in her eyes, happy tears. I start to cry too.

She drops me off at the motel parking lot on her way home.

"I don't want to see you home again until the morning. And you better have a few black and blue marks and rope burns when you show up!" she instructs. "Now, go and do unspeakable things with that man."

I smile and wave as she pulls out of the parking lot.

CHAPTER TWENTY-FOUR

I knock timidly on Chaim's room door and wait. He opens the door. He blinks at me in complete surprise, then holds the door open wide and beckons me into his room. He's on his cell.

"Yes, I have plenty. Yes, undershirts too. I won't have to wash any out for days. I'm eating fine, you shouldn't worry. Thanks for the brisket sandwiches."

His mother.

I glance around the room. It's modern and simple. Chaim has managed to find the adult movie channel, which is on mute. As he chats with his mother, he goes into the bathroom and begins running a bath. He ends his call and returns.

"Anatevka, what a surprise! Where is your *mameleh*?"

Did he think I would bring my mother with me? *Oy vey.*

"She went home. I came to talk."

"Just to talk, *tsatskeleh*?"

"We need to talk more. We just *shtup* and when we talk, we talk about *shtupping*."

"Okay, so we'll talk. What do you want we should talk about?"

"Something really meaningful and profound. You know."

"As always, Miss Stein, you surprise me. You start."

Hmm…. A rare opportunity, must not waste it.

"What's your favorite movie?" I ask.

"Between you and me? *Yentl*. 'Papa can you hear me?' That song makes me cry. And Barbra Streisand as a *yeshiva bocher*—*Oy*, if they were all like that, I could go for little boys."

My Chaim! I love this man.

"I also like this movie *The Secretary*, with the typing and the spanking. I've seen it, oh, twelve times. Little Chaim gets such a thrill whenever I even think about it. And you, *tsatskeleh*?"

"I really liked *Twilight*. And *Twilight: New Moon*. Also *Twilight: Eclipse*. I very much enjoyed *Twilight: Breaking Dawn*."

"Ah, Ana, you fascinate me. I've never met anyone like you."

He touches my face with his pudgy fingers, nearly poking me in the eye. Oh my. I get a whiff of his unique Chaim smell. Sweat, gravy and horseradish. I guess he's not using the body wash I bought him.

"This conversation has really helped me," I whisper. "I think we could *shtup* now."

"Yes, Anatevka," he breathes. "You and I, we both want the same things. Let's *shtup*."

My breath hitches. My skin flushes. In the room next door, a toilet flushes.

"There is one thing…. It's that time of month."

I don't know why I didn't think of this. I know this is a big deal for Orthodox Jews. They hate this. A menstruating wife is forbidden to go near her husband. Chaim is going to flip out. What if he spanks me?

"You're bleeding? *Niddah*?"

Oh no. I nod fearfully.

"Yes, a little. I guess that means I'm off limits."

"Bleeding, shmeeding, this is great. Now we can skip the condoms! Come to me, my beautiful little unclean one."

Oh Chaim! Always so sweet.

He leads me into the bathroom. The sink vanity is covered with shaving gear, creams and powders, bottles of pills, nasal sprays, ace bandages, gauze, hot and cold packs, a flashlight, PVC tape, an AM/FM radio, a hammer, rubber gloves, a hacksaw, an oxygen tank, and a portable defibrillator.

"A few things I like to travel with," he explains. "Just in case."

Chaim has so many issues.

The small acrylic bathtub is full and he turns the tap off. Around the lip, I see the hotel soaps, shampoo and conditioner, and a small yellow rubber duck, complete with yarmulke and *tallit*.

"I take that with me too," Chaim says. "For luck."

It's warm in the tiny bathroom. He begins to undress me from behind. There isn't much room. I'm squeezed between the porcelain knobs of the vanity and Chaim's own porcelain knob.

"I'm going to *shtup* you here in the bathroom, Anastasia."

He kisses my neck. I slouch to make it easier for him. He pulls down my pants and panties and I step out of them.

"You are one hot Jewess," he says, groping and fondling me like a melon. I gasp and whimper, like a melon having an orgasm.

"Yes, *tsatskeleh*, yes, let yourself go," he urges. His voice is thin and nasal.

I writhe in ecstasy as he starts undressing in front of me. It takes him a while. First the lace-up shoes. Then his dark three-piece suit. Then his white button-down shirt. Fortunately, as always, there is no necktie. Then his *tzitzit*, his undershirt and his baggy boxer shorts. Then the long socks with garters.

When he's finally done, the bathroom is crammed with clothing and accessories, not to mention the survival gear and emergency medical supplies. There's no more room to writhe in ecstasy.

He tugs on the string between my legs, pulls out the Tampon, and puts it on the sink.

"Ana, promise me you'll save this and turn it into a *kabbalah* string," he murmurs. "It would mean a lot to me."

"Oh Chaim, I promise," I pant.

He holds my hand as I step into the bathtub. Then he follows and as he does, I once again see the pattern of scars on his chest. What could have caused this? The suspense is killing me. Is he really going to wait until the sequel to tell me?

It's a tight fit in the tub. He sits and lowers me into his lap, facing away from him. I feel him deep inside me. It's as if we were one. His thighs press against mine, pushing them into the side of the tub. The fit is extremely tight. Painfully tight. Clasping the ledge and soap tray, I try to move up and down but I can't. There is squeaking but little movement. We are stuck.

"*Tsatskseleh*, my hip. Could be a cramp. Or it's dislocated. *Oy gevalt!*"

We try to push ourselves out of the tub but it's no good.

"Can you find the soap?" I ask. The soap and the Jewish rubber duck have fallen in.

"Hey, this is no time to wash," he says, testily. "I'm in pain here."

I explore the sudsy water with my hands and grab the soap, clamping onto it tightly with my fingernails so I don't lose it.

"That's not the soap!" Chaim yelps.

Finally, I find the small slippery bar and use it to soap my thighs and the side of the tub. The suction still holds us in place but there is movement. I push upward and forward and, suddenly, with a whoosh, I am free. Chaim remains in the tub, inert, numbed by the pressure on his joints and muscles.

"*Oy*, do I need a doctor," he moans.

Slowly, I am able to raise him from the tub. I dry him off and lead him to bed, where we both collapse with relief. Just before I close my eyes, I think about my Mom. Then I think about my conversation with Chaim. I realize I've never been happier.

CHAPTER TWENTY-FIVE

Chaim stands in a steel-barred cage. He is wearing his trademark dark pants, but his belly is majestically, spherically, humongously, bare, and he's smirking. He has a platter of bagels in his hands. He pads up to the front of the cage. Holding up a plump bagel, he extends one hand through the bars.

"Eat, Ana. There are people starving in Africa. Eat, Ana. Eat," Chaim says. His words echo eerily because this is a dream sequence.

I try to move toward the bagel but I am unable to. I am held back by something at my ankles, a knotted silk prayer shawl.

"I can't reach you, Chaim. I'm being prevented by some very deep symbolism."

I grab at the bagel and, just as suddenly as it's in my hand, it's gone.

"Wake up, *tsatskeleh*. We have a big day ahead."

It's Chaim, not in a cage, but hovering over me like a Macy's Thanksgiving Day Parade balloon.

"Good morning, *tsatskeleh*."

"No, please," I plead. "It's 5AM. I need to sleep." I want to go back to my bagel dream and find out how it ends.

"I want to ride a roller coaster with you," he says, kissing me gently. I open my eyes.

Oh no, I think. I'm not familiar with the expression "ride a roller coaster" but I'm too tired for anything right now, let alone kink.

"We can't have morning sex until the morning," I complain wearily.

"Not sex. I want you should get dressed. We have to get going."

"Okay, okay."

I clamber off the bed and look for my clothes. Then I clamber into to the bathroom where I quickly wash up, then clamber out. I clamber onto a chair to put on my hose, then clambering off the chair to finish dressing. Finally, I'm done clambering.

"Ready!" I announce.

Chaim offers me a cup of coffee and a glazed donut from the free breakfast bar in the lobby. My heart sings! So caring. I am loved. Free donuts? The people who run the Hampton Inn are the best. Will I ever get enough of this hotel chain?

Within minutes we are on the road.

"What are we doing?"

"It's a surprise."

"Where are we going?"

"You'll see. Trust me."

Oy vey.

As we drive, the sound of a thousand violins whines through the car's tinny speakers.

"What are we listening to?" I ask.

"'*Va Pensiero*' from *Nabucco*. It's an opera by Verdi. You shouldn't think I'm always a *bovan*."

"I'm impressed," I smirk. "I didn't know you liked opera. What's it about?"

"It's the Chorus of the Hebrew Slaves. They're in chains. What's not to like?"

He smirks at me. I'm about to smirk back when he smirks again. Damn. I've been out-smirked.

"Not your taste, *tsatskeleh*?"

He turns the music off. In the silence, he starts humming a song from Fiddler on the Roof.

> *"If I were a rich man*
> *I-I sti-ill wouldn't be-ee*
> *Aa-as ri-ich aa-as me.*
> *Yiddle-diddle-daidle-diddle*
> *Yiddle-diddle-daidle-dee.*

My Chaim. He's so lovable when he's like this.

We pull off the highway into a small town with street lamps that look like Chocolate Kisses. I must still be back in my dream.

"Where are we?" I ask.

"Hershey, Pennsylvania."

"Why?"

I've been hoping Chaim might start watching his calories. Hershey? No!

We pull into a large parking lot in an amusement park!

"I told you, we're going to ride a roller coaster."

"So that's not a kind of sex? It's a real roller coaster?"

"*Oy*, my little *lokshen*, don't be a wisenheimer or I'll take you over my knee."

Chaim buys tickets and leads me into the park to a sign that says, *skyrush*. Sounds Russian. Oh wait, it's *sky rush*. Standing patiently in line is Schneider, saving a spot for us. The people behind him are not pleased as we take his place.

"Hello, Schneider," I utter sweetly.

Does Chaim do anything without Schneider? From dry-cleaning to amusement parks, he's a one-man Israeli Defense Force.

"*Shalom*, Miss Stein," he replies, courteously. "Enjoy your ride!"

"Ana," Chaim summons me. "Come."

He is speaking to the ride attendant.

"This is my girlfriend, Ana, who will be accompanying me. We're both over sixty inches tall."

He called me his girlfriend! A real breakthrough and so unexpected. And he's sixty inches tall? Today is full of good news.

The attendant grunts and lets us through. The roller coaster is long, sleek, and yellow with blue plastic seats.

We clamber onto our seats.

"Again with the clambering," Chaim says. "Now we need to strap you in."

I'm about to pull down the restraint that would hold me in my seat when Chaim stops me.

"I'll do that," he says sternly, and slowly pulls the harness over my head and down onto my lap.

"You really like restraining me," I smirk.

"You should only know," he says, his breathing suddenly very short. He grabs hold of the metal restraining bar. "Ooooh... Ana."

What just happened? Geez.

"I never figured you for a roller coaster buff. You don't even like to fly."

Score one for Ana.

"What can I say? Hearing people shriek in terror relaxes me. At least we never leave the ground."

He's so animated and happy now. Creepy too, but definitely happy.

"Ana," he murmurs softly, and looks at me seriously, his glassy black eyes piercing my soul.

"Yes, Chaim?" I murmur back.

"You may experience unexpected, rapid changes in speed, direction, and/or elevation. Long hair, headscarves and long jewelry must be secured. Loose articles not physically attached to you may not be taken on this ride."

I love this man.

The roller coaster starts. Slowly, we climb the first steep slope until we reach the peak.

"Here we go, *tsatskeleh*."

And suddenly we are plummeting to Earth as if we are in free-fall. My heart is in my mouth. Holy Moses—it's awesome.

I can see why he wanted to do this. Just Chaim and I, testing the laws of physics, the sun and wind in our faces, hundreds of screaming people ahead of and behind us.

"Spectacular!" I say to him.

"Look, you can see Sidney Cha-Cha from here!" he says as the parking lot comes into view.

We whip from curve to curve, climbing and falling, falling and climbing. It's like we're having sex. And then, in two minutes, it's over. Yes, it's exactly like we're having sex.

Back at the starting point, I take a deep breath while Chaim releases my restraints.

"Was it good for you, *tsatskeleh*?" he murmurs, and his eyes are pools of dark black.

"Incredible," I gasp.

"Come." He holds out his hand for me, and I clamber out of the roller coaster. "We need some cotton candy."

CHAPTER TWENTY-SIX

Chaim drives me back to my Mother's and heads back to Brooklyn alone in haste. A crisis at one of his bagel plants. Before leaving, he curses into his cell phone.

"All Senior Executives in my office in an hour—Goldie, Lou, Sol, Max, Ida, Leo. You should all have pains in your bowels for this! No one goes home until I get answers."

Heavy lies the head that wears the *yarmulke*.

I pack my things as my Mom watches.

"I'm happy the two of you had a good time," she says. "He would make such a good first husband."

Her voice is choked with emotion. My Mom really does want me to be happy.

Thinking of Chaim, I feel a little weepy too. I'm finally a grown-up! Oh, Mom! Oh, Mr. Pinkerton! I marvel at the bond I have with this dear, sweet stuffed animal. He and I share a warm, pink fuzzy hug. Then my Mom drives me to the bus stop.

"So we'll talk again soon, honey? Don't blow this."

"Yes, Mom."

> From: Anatevka Stein
> Subject: Brooklyn Bound (and Gagged)
> Date: June 8 2013 12:15
> To: Chaim Silver
>
> Hope your bagel crisis is under control.
> Am heading to the GW Bridge. ETA your
> place in approximately 90 minutes. Can't
> wait.
>
> Your Ana

> From: Chaim Silver
> Subject: Brooklyn Bound (and Gagged)
> Date: June 8 2013 12:20
> To: Anatevka Stein
>
> Thanks for letting me know. See you
> soon.
>
> Chaim Silver
> CEO, Silver Bagels Holdings Dot Com
> Limited Inc.

Now I'm worried. So short and perfunctory.

Where's the lust, the kink, the drooling perversity?
Something must really be wrong.

> From: Anatevka Stein
> Subject: Brooklyn Bound
> Date: June 8 2013 12:25
> To: Chaim Silver
>
> Dearest Mr. Silver
>
> Are you okay? You don't sound well.
>
> Your Ana

> From: Chaim Silver
> Subject: Brooklyn Bound
> Date: June 8 2013 12:29
> To: Anatevka Stein
>
> Everything is fine, my needy little
> *knaidlach*. Nothing that an over-the-knee
> spanking and a painfully large butt-plug
> can't fix. Keep your panties on… until
> you get here.
>
> Laters, *tsatskeleh*!
>
> Chaim Silver
> CEO, Silver Bagels Technology Holdings
> Dot Com Limited, Inc.

Oy vey. That's more like it. Now everything will be okay.

Chaim's apartment is quiet and eerily empty as I enter—except for faint notes from his accordion. How I love to watch and listen as he plays. I slip into the living room, trying not to disturb him. He looks up as I enter.

"Don't stop, please," I plead. "What is it? It's beautiful."

I've been studying up on music, and this sounds like Bach or Handel or maybe Purcell.

"'You Light Up My Life,'" he murmurs.

"You're sweet. You light up mine too."

"No, that's the name of the song. Debby Boone you've heard of, maybe? You don't know it?"

I shake my head. The music is beautiful. So many nights I'd sit by my window, waiting for someone to sing me his song. And now I have Chaim. He fills up my night with song. He gives me hope, to carry on.

But then he stops.

He gets up and shuffles toward me, his face contorted with desire, a tiny bit of toasted bagel on his chin. He grabs me needfully, his tongue swirling in my mouth like a propeller. He grabs my buttocks, squeezing them over and over, panting, "*Oy*, such a *tuches!*" I smell his Chaim smell—fish, sour cream, and unwashed laundry. Still not using the body wash.

"Why do you only play such soulful music?" I ask.

"I threw myself into learning the accordion after Jewish summer camp."

"To take away the pain?"

"Yes, to help me forget."

"Do you want to talk about it?"

"I can think of other things I'd rather do. To you, *tsatskeleh*, baby, and your *tuches*!"

He smirks devilishly. Ooh, what he does to me. My stomach clenches. My heart clenches. My jaw clenches. My fist clenches. I try to clench my toes, but it's no use. I'm officially out of things to clench.

"And what would those other things be?" I ask shyly.

"Ach, never mind. You wouldn't like it."

"Like what?"

"*Oy*, the things I'd do to you!"

"Show me," I tell him.

"What? I've already told you and shown you. You don't know yet? I should take out an ad in *The New York Times* maybe?"

"Oh. Right. Sadism, humiliation, abuse.... Well, show me anyway, so I can be shocked and appalled yet strangely turned on all over again, like it's all a complete surprise."

"*Oy vey*, if you say so."

We get up and he leads me once again to the Blue Room of Broadloom.

CHAPTER TWENTY-SEVEN

I am dressed in my *balaboosta* costume—pullover shirt, long skirt, hair covering, heavy stockings. My inner yenta is making chicken soup. I am cowering as I wait for Chaim to enter. What will he do? What sacrilegious fantasy will we enact? Will his back give out? What if it's his heart? Sheesh, I hope not. A Hatzollah ambulance would come and I'd have to explain all this to a team of Orthodox EMTs.

The door opens and Chaim walks in. He's wearing a wide-brimmed black hat, black gabardine jacket, and dark gray pants. Except this time they're knickers, and he's wearing white silk stockings below the knee. He's dressed like an Eighteenth Century hasid. This is serious.

Chaim winds a black handkerchief around my eyes and ties it behind me. Then he places a pair of giant headphones on my head. I feel like an air traffic controller.

"This is so you can't see or hear me," he says. "You can only feel me."

And smell you? Will Chaim ever wear the body wash I bought him?

"You will hear only music."

He begins to undress me. It takes a while, as my uniform is heavy and there is lots of it. It feels great to be out of it though. When I am naked, he gently guides me to the bed. I lie on my stomach as he shackles my hands and feet to the four posters at the corners.

My heart is beating like a steel drum at a destination wedding.

"Wait just a minute," he says. "I need to turn on the music."

Will it be Barry Manilow? Barbra Streisand? No, not this time.

"Quiet, now, *tsatskeleh*."

I hear the sound of a phonograph needle landing on a vinyl LP, then the familiar snap and crackle of an old recording.

A lone mournful voice sings unaccompanied, almost sobbing. I have never heard anything so depressing. At the same time, I feel something on my back. It's Chaim's hand, but encased in something—an oven mitt? He's touching me with it, everywhere.

Chaim moves the oven mitt down my body, below my belly button, between my legs, then down my thighs and legs. I am completely at his mercy.

The sad, scratchy music is still playing. I manage to make out "My Yiddishe Mama."

"What is this music?" I ask.

"'Yossele Rosenblatt Live,'" he tells me. "No one sang 'My Yiddishe Mama' like him. Though I like Jackie Wilson's version too, and he was a *schvartze*. Go know."

Suddenly he climbs onto the bed. I feel his weight next to me as he starts spanking my rear end.

"*Oy* this tushy—so soft yet so firm. I'm going to spank you now, hard. First with my hand. Then with a belt. And then with a rusty iron pipe I found on the street. You tell me if it hurts."

The spanking begins and it definitely hurts. The hand not so much, the belt some, but I think the rusty metal pipe is getting to me. I can't take too much more.

"It hurts," I say.

"It what?" he answers, hitting me again.

"It hurts," I say again, but he doesn't stop.

"I'm not quite understanding you," he says. "It must be your pronunciation."

"It hoits," I say, and finally he stops.

Thank *G-d*.

"That's my Anatevka," he whispers. "You really took a lot of punishment, sweetie. Sorry about the rusty pipe. You're going to need a tetanus shot. Now, turn over."

He unlocks the shackles holding me to the bed but locks them again once I am on my back.

Oh no, what happens now?

Then the tickling begins. It comes hard, under my armpits and down my ribcage. I can't control my limbs. The sensation is too much for me.

"Stop squirming!" he commands.

"I can't," I giggle at him.

The torment is excruciating. He tickles me further, behind my knees and in the crook of my elbows.

I try to hold on to sanity. I am overwhelmed, yet he does not stop. Not behind my ears! Tears spring unwelcome into my eyes. He's not holding anything back. And then, oh no—my belly button! I weep uncontrollably.

Finally, he is finished. I am still struggling against the restraints as he undoes them.

"Don't touch me!" I hiss. "You promised, no tickling!"

"When did I promise?"

"In the contract. Months ago. I insisted."

"But I didn't... we hadn't signed... Ana, please!"

"Don't give me legalisms. I said no tickling and I meant it. Nobody tickles Anatevka Stein!"

I run from the Blue Room of Broadloom to the

bedroom and close the door behind me. I wrap my arms around myself. *Oy!* Thank *G-d*, the feeling is fading. How could I have been so foolish? Why did I let him do that to me? Spanking, whipping, sure. Maybe a golden shower, some fisting, a little asphyxiation. Different strokes. I wanted to experience the dark side, to know how bad it could be, but it's too dark for me. So that's how Chaim really gets his kicks. Tickling! I cannot do it. Not now, not ever.

CHAPTER TWENTY-EIGHT

What a wake-up call this has been. True, he warned me, but did he warn me enough? Ten times? Twenty? He should have tried harder. And why did I listen to my mother? "Follow your libido?" Right, and what did it get me? Tickled nearly into a coma.

But can I live without Chaim? I was just beginning to get used to him, his style, his singsong voice, his unique aroma.

The door opens. It's him.

"Some Klonapin," he says after a long while, "for your nerves. To take the edge off. And for your injuries, some antibiotics."

I gaze at his rotund face.

In such a short time, he's become so, so dear to me. Reaching up, I run my fingers along his jowls and caress his chins.

"I'm sorry," I whisper.

"I am sorry I tickled you."

"That's okay. At least now I know. I'm not for you."

"*Tsatkseleh*, what are you saying?"

"It's what you need, you said so. Now I know what you like. But it's too much. I can't be with a man who would want to see me squirming and giggling like that."

"*Oy vey*, so we'll skip the tickling. There's so much else we can share. Hot wax, leashes, infantilization…."

"I don't want to leave. I love you," I tell him. "But I can't stay."

"I don't want you to go," he answers. "I've come alive since I met you. I need you. Little Chaim needs you."

Uh oh. I try not to look below his belt.

"I have to go."

"No you don't have to go."

"I should."

"You shouldn't."

"This exchange is pointless and repetitive," I tell him.

"No it's not pointless and repetitive."

"I need to get dressed. And don't tell me I don't need to get dressed."

I find my clothes and put them on. Wandering

through Chaim's home I see the room where, only hours before, I had sat rapt as he played the accordion. So much has happened since then. I've seen so much during my descent into the depths of depravity. I love him, but I cannot be with him. I place the old MacBook and the keys to the Hyundai on the night table. I write him a short note.

> Chaim,
>
> I love you but *oy vey* are you creepy. I can't take it anymore.
>
> Good-bye. Maybe things will be different in the sequel.
>
> Anatevka

I manage to get home. I sit on my bed and howl. The ache is indescribable. After all that spanking, I should have known better than to sit down anywhere. So much pain—in my heart, in my soul, and most of all, all over my tushy. I curl up in the fetal position and wonder. Can I live without Chaim? Will I ever love again? How long before I can use my desk chair?

BONUS PREVIEW

An excerpt from the sequel, *Volume Two: Fifty Shades Meshuggener*

"Here." Chaim hands me a Mont Blanc fountain pen. "I got this at my bar mitzvah," he tells me gravely.

"What do you want me to do with it?" I ask. "It's a little late to write thank you notes."

"Don't be a wisenheimer," he answers. "I want you to connect the dots."

He takes off his shirt, and I see what he means. I clamber over to him. He takes my hand and guides it over the mound of his belly. We begin drawing fine ink lines on his chest, across and back, up and down, between his man boobs, slowly tracing the path of his scars. There are six distinct points and several sharp angles. When we are done, I see the pattern clearly for the first time: The Star of David.

But how did the scars get there? Surgery? Rough sex gone wrong? Jewish industrial accident? No, it must be something worse, much worse. Could it be? I shudder as the realization hits me. There's really only one likely explanation. After giving him an atomic wedgie, the bullies at his Jewish summer camp painted his chest with a peanut butter Star of David, and then chased him into the woods where he was attacked by famished, peanut butter-loving squirrels.

I can picture it as vividly as if it were happening at that exact moment. Chaim frightened, crying, his underwear stretched to its limit, his chest coated with the sticky peanut butter. Furry woodland creatures clawing and biting. *Oy vey!*

With my eyes, I let him see that I know the truth.

"Yes, it was a vicious attack," he says quietly. "They were on me in an instant. I was lucky not to get rabies, though I had to get shots. Since then, I don't like to be touched on my chest."

"I'll bet you can't eat peanut butter either," I say, as soothingly as I can.

"No," he says, "food is food. I love peanut butter, especially on matzah at Passover."

My Chaim!

"So now you know," he says, solemnly.

"Yes." I nuzzle him. "And it was so worth waiting for the sequel to find out."

BONUS BONUS PREVIEW

An excerpt from the sequel to the sequel, *Volume III: Fifty Shades Fried Latkes: The Prequel*

"Chaim, come and help us light the Menorah!"

It's my Mom. She is making latkes. I love latkes. There is a big menorah in the dining room. Each night we light candles. Each night we add a candle. After eight nights, there will be no more room to add candles. Then we will stop. No more candles, no more Hanukkah, no more latkes.

I like latkes. But I have found something I like even better.

"Mom, will you tell him to hurry up? I need to use the bathroom and it's been half an hour!"

That's Mischa, my sister. She is always knocking on the door, telling me to hurry up. What does she need the bathroom for?

"Again with the bathroom? What's with that boy?

Ever since he came back from camp, always in the bathroom. Chaim, are you constipated? I think you need to see your pediatrician."

That's my Dad. He's always aggravated.

"Leave him alone. I'll give him some prunes after dinner, he'll be regular."

My Mom is always giving me prunes. I'm not constipated. I just need to be left alone to think. I am thinking of summer camp. Those boys were very mean to me, but putting me in the infirmary was the best thing ever. Because I met the nurse, Mrs. Rosenberg. She taught me things. Exciting things. She made me feel like a man.

"Chaim, come out of there!" It's my sister again, banging on the door. "And stop using up all my moisturizer! It's not for acne!"

But I'm not using it for acne. I put the last of Mischa's moisturizer in my palm. Poor Mischa. My mind travels far away. I am in the infirmary with Mrs. Rosenberg. My hand is her hand. She is touching me. No, Mrs. Rosenberg. I don't think you should be touching me there, Mrs. Rosenberg. Wait... please... Mrs. Rosenberg! Ohhhh... ahhhhhhhh.

That was good. No, it was great! Better than latkes. But I like latkes too. I wash up and unlock the door. Time to light the candles. My father is aggravated. Mischa is glowering. My mother is worried.

There's a dreidel on the table. It has the Hebrew letters nun, hay, gimmel *and* shin *on it. They stand for*

E L JAMESBERGSTEIN

"A great miracle happened here." Yes, it did. It really did.

Happy Hanukkah, Mrs. Rosenberg. Happy Hanukkah to me.

ABOUT THE AUTHOR

E.L. Jamesbergstein is a writer and *balaboosta* based in Brooklyn, New York. From early childhood, she dreamed of creating stories that readers would fall in love with, but put those dreams on hold to write this book. She is currently working on a Jewish cookbook for vampires.

30824759R00102

Made in the USA
Middletown, DE
07 April 2016